MAD LANDS
THE COMPLETE ANTHOLOGY

'The Symphony of Adam Apocalypse'
Written by
Joseph Dawson

'Tales from The Animated Assembly Vol.1'
Written by
Sonia Kurach
Joseph Dawson

For professional and amateur performing rights and all other production related enquiries, please get in touch using the email below.

Production Email:
AnimatedAssemblyTheatreCompany@gmail.com

Animated Assembly Theatre Company Ltd. is a London based Production Company that was born out of a collaborative group formed in 2019 by a team of students at London Metropolitan University. Utilising what began life as an extracurricular project to learn vital skills to support their studies, 'Infamia: Empires in America' paved the way for 'The Graphic Theatre Company' to be born, where it remained under the aforementioned name until its incorporation and subsequent name change in the summer of 2020 to 'Animated Assembly Theatre Company Ltd.'

In addition to developing productions for both Theatre and Film. AATC is a company led by core philosophies in delivering performative, visceral and expressionistic work which seeks to explore and deconstruct 'genre' as it relates to storytelling. The company, although in its infancy, is heavily engaged in developing its own practical research into exploring performativity and how the traversal between such states is dependent upon genre, style and convention. The company has been approached to contribute to multiple international projects, all thanks to the efforts of a collaborative team of incredibly talented and dedicated artists.

MADLANDS: THE COMPLETE ANTHOLOGY contains scenes of strong violence, psychological terror, terminologies and ideologies which some readers may find disturbing or offensive. You have been warned...

There he dances, there he dances, as if a master, to the candle in the wind. Yearning wildly and always, to sail amongst starlight. For the world beneath his wanderings was as nefarious to him as it had been for all mankind.

In his journeys, there were strange tides upon stranger shores. Upon a dying world, stood a city built into the heart of a shining star, burning with more vibrant beauty than the wonderous magnificence of a thousand rainbows, and there was merriment in the end. Consumed by lights and then rendered silent in the ghost fields, stretching into the dry mountains for a thousand years.

In other places, there were green trees, a churning forest floor, wet and mud ridden amber leaves, a whispering orchestra, stirring in the dark. Conducting their feet, each in their own way, soon to be separated for all time, were children in chainmail, playing at war when they themselves had never known peace.

There were monsters amongst them that wore the skins of men to frighten the children, many ran, few remained, and few died.

Of those that fled beyond the eye of the horizon, soon enough their terror turned them to tears, and their tears turned them to dust, bittersweet imaginings scattered by him, who dances as if a master to the candle in the wind.

Once upon a time, there was a country ruled and made by children. The pinnacle of their imagination forged a city that never permitted bedtime, for to rest was to resign to decay, in their own minds, the mortal had not time for humility.

4

In moments, there were many years, and many regrets.

Infinitely blossoming, parables, formed out of necessity, spat upon white shores with droplets of blood. When at last there was peace, others came along the night sky, children of patchwork quilting, following nothing other an unexpected calling on an unwanted wind.

Before he who danced could dance once more, he realised he had waned in his wanderings, thus, in the end, there was nothing more he could do, no further place he could run. And with his dying breath he called out for the world to let roam free the brave cavalry of humankind.

This is another world, a world of consequence.

Yours sincerely,
Joseph George Dawson.

P.S

Thank you to my editor, Lauren. For burning your hands this past year to help me catch fire in a bottle.

CONTENTS

'PARABLES OF PERSPECTIVE' An introduction by Joseph Dawson. Pg.7

THE SYMPHONY OF ADAM APOCALYPSE:

Movement I: Birth. Pg.17

Movement II: Hope. Pg.64

Movement III: Responsibility. Pg.99

Movement IV: Regret. Pg.152

TALES FROM THE ANIMATED ASSEMBLY VOL.1:

I: Don't Play with Fire. Pg. 179

II: The Children of War. Pg. 185

III: Kubrick, my love. Pg. 190

IV: Italian American Payphone Story. Pg. 196

V: Interstellar Imperium. Pg. 201

VI: A provoking Letter. Pg. 204

VII: Everyman. Pg. 207

PARABLES OF PERSPECTIVE

An Introduction by Joseph Dawson.

A Parable is defined by Cambridge English Dictionary as "A short, simple story that teaches or explains an idea, especially a moral or religious idea." While to my colleagues and close friends, the words "Short." and "Simple." would not lend themselves well in relation to a general description of my work. There is always undoubtedly an emphasis upon a particular moral philosophy in all of my stories.

In my first published work 'Infamia: Empires in America' I explored through the common literary devices of analogy and personification, my own childhood. Told through the course of an epic story surrounding Italian American organised crime figures in New York City during the 1930's. Of course, there was a historically accurate foundation to support the 'spine' of my work. The nature of creating a genuine depiction of a historical period in narrative, even if abundant in fictitious elements, requires at least a thematic honouring of the period itself.

When asked, I have always described the play of 'Infamia' as something more akin to a Spaghetti Western rather than a true 'Mob Epic'. Be it Anatolio's rejection of power, Enzo's redemption arc or even Fierce Valentino's anti heroism in the finale of the work. There are many elements which would perhaps be more commonly found in a Western than a Mafia story.

The world which began with 'Infamia' quickly became the canonical foundation for all the stories which have followed since. Although the publishing of this Anthology is my second public work, it is by no means a reflection of the total number of works I have written.

My reasoning for creating this 'Theatreverse' of plays, the collection of which I have titled 'The Theatre of Consequence' stems from my original desire to develop analogical stories in the form of novels. I had an aspiration to create a world for my stories that could, in time, aspire to share the same level of complexity as that of J.R.R Tolkien's Middle Earth.

My exploration of Theatre following my departure from The British Army may have changed the conduit of which my larger vision of a dangerous world ruled by consequence is executed. However, that raw ambition, to deliver stories which analogise my own life experiences, with some form of an extrapolated meaning or sense of 'closure' that is both relevant to myself and the audience, is still very much being satisfied.

This anthology explores many themes in its various stories and writings, though if I were to generalise the entire contents of this book under one theme or idea. I would most certainly choose the word 'Perspective' to best encapsulate this gallery of mad ramblings. Many Psychologists, Philosophers and Poets have studied and written of 'The Universal Human Experience' that in which we all share. Heartbreak, nostalgia, laughter and remorse are merely footnotes in an ever ephemeral yet ever eternal collective story which reprises itself with each passing generation, and will do so, likely, till the end of our time.

In light of The Coronavirus Pandemic which has swept the world, there have been many whose lives have been irreparably altered by this single event, their entire perspective upon life changed. It is quite right that tragedy should change a person. All of us endure significant tragedies in our lives, and there are many more which seem to fall by the wayside if they fail to meet the severity of their significant counterparts.

Perhaps this is because the term 'tragedy' is not often treated as being relative to the individual, instead, there is an almost mythical aura of objectivity surrounding the term. Thus, many of us feel guilty for suffering that which we endure. "Remember, there's always someone more worse for wear than yourself." Offers little respite.

Considering that tragedy is relative to the individual experience, it isn't then, wild to suggest that a tragic event, with enough severity to destabilise ordinary patterns of daily routine, might in itself be considered a truly apocalyptic event at the personal level. Many find comfort (sometimes at the risk of a satisfying existence) in predicable patterns of daily routine, with enough room to diversify activity and avoid insanity. It does not take long for a person to fall under the illusion of a supposed permanence as it relates to daily living.

Yet, in particular cases, those of which often become parables in their own right. An apocalyptic event may strike and the individual who only a short time ago was utterly secured in their existence, now finds their entire state of reality in tatters. Finding oneself in such a state would be bad enough, if not for the aggravating sense of blindness on the part of individuals who, despite being only a few inches away from the tragedy, are entirely unaffected by the death of paradise. A tragedy of such severity breeds a dangerous existential crisis, one that can be incredibly isolating and ultimately self-destructive.

As someone who has lived through multiple significant tragedies in his life, I have become very familiar with this 'crisis of perspective' My parent's violent marriage and the fragmentation of a very toxic family environment, through malicious divorce proceedings, had left me feeling incredibly out of place in the world, even from an early age.

Had I not been so young during the time of divorce and therefore 'unaware' enough to adjust to the constant vindictive arrangements between my parents, I think the impacts of both having observed and been a victim of consistent domestic abuse at the hands of my mother, would've had a far more immediately profound effect. Arguably more preferable, than laying in wait till my mid-teens, when the inevitable confrontations that were long overdue, began to erupt.

While it can be argued that 'change' is a simple fact of life, I believe there are methods of change which are better than others, a radical introduction to a new reality is bound to leave scar tissue than merely offer a gradual adjustment and acceptance to a different way of living. Having enlisted in The British Army at the age of sixteen, however unsteady my life had been up to that point, it wasn't for many years that I knew my first personal era of peace.

I don't like to talk about my experiences in the army, at least not those which have unfortunately seemed to define me far more than the many wonderous adventures, of which I shared with some of the bravest young men whom I have ever known. Returning to the world from those experiences, both the good and bad, was incredibly difficult for me. The sheer weight of my childhood, once held within the buildings, the fields and the shores of my hometown, was somehow lightened, for all that seemed to remain, was shadows upon every corner.

I was not aware of how much the grime of the real world had changed me. To the few familiar faces that remained to greet me, I was unrecognisable. And to me, they were unbearable. There are still times, though rarer with each passing year, even amongst good friends and warm conversation, where I cannot help but isolate myself from ordinary life. In those early days, I gravitated towards Tolkien's words "There is no going back." As I was expected by all those around me to somehow live an ordinary life, when in all honesty, I had never known such a thing.

It has been a surreal experience, as a young man, to see shocked eyes on wearier faces than mine, when I tell brief extracts of my story. Perhaps that is why I'm so attracted to the outrageous, the uncommon and the strange, for an unconscious personal pursuit of normality.

The knowledge of finality as it relates to love and friendship has made me appreciate the smallest things, the strange little stories of peoples' everyday lives. You need not look as far as you would think to hear the greatest story ever told. That which comprises even the most magnificent tale, lives and breathes all around us.

Eventually, I left my home for the second time, and have never returned since. Despite my always altering perspective upon life being a major advantage to finding the passion and patience to write, in search of a cathartic treasure, I suppose. There are times where there is simply too much that offers too little to find. I expect it will be many years before I am able to return, having spent a great deal of time estranged from my entire family, even despite reconnecting with my father, I consider myself as alone as I have always been. Though, you must understand, it is not a purely terrible thing, rather, I cherish the freedom on most days.

To know I could set off across the world tomorrow, without a care nor consequence on my tail, that is a beautiful thing. Although it is far from a perfect one, it is a most adventurous life. 'The Symphony of Adam Apocalypse' being my major contribution to this book, is a story that explores how radical changes in the perception of reality can lead one into darkness, danger and disillusionment. It is an existential experience, a play of four visions.

I have been grateful to work with many of my talented colleagues at The Animated Assembly Theatre Company on bringing this work to life in a dedicated developmental project throughout the course of 2020. Adding their unique voices to these pages.

In retrospect of what has been almost an entire year spent upon the creation of this collection, I have come to terms with many things which once upon a time, I would have either refused or been unable to accept. It is not to say that the work is done, I suspect it will a very long time before I am able to make peace with all of it. Yet, for all that it has cost, the conflict between then and now, between the ephemeral and the eternal, it has created a world in my mind, in which the possibilities are truly limitless. And that is an encouraging thought.

In the end, I suppose we are subject to our own perspectives upon the strangeness of life, we are both always and never alone. We are each walking our own roads, in our own time, and while two roads may be identical, they are never truly the same. I believe, at whatever point on our road we may find ourselves, we must remember that a stumble, no matter how severe, does not condemn the remainder of the journey, in good time, the view becomes quite extraordinary.

Project 'Symphony' oversaw the practical development of 'Movement III' and the literary development of the entire work thereafter.

THE ANIMATED ASSEMBLY THEATRE COMPANY

PROJECT 'SYMPHONY' 2020

PRODUCTION CREDITS:

JOSEPH DAWSON: Artistic Director. Author of 'The Symphony of Adam Apocalypse' Curator and Co-Author of 'Tales from The Animated Assembly Vol. 1'.

AKULINA RUGOJEVA: Project Producer. Makeup Artist.

DANIELA BERTUZZI: Set, Prop and Costume Designer.

OLEKSIY ANDRONYAK: Director of Photography, Video Production.

LAUREN TILLBROOK: Script Dramaturg, Editor and Dramaturg of 'Madlands: The Complete Anthology'.

THOMAS GREENFIELD: Script Dramaturg.

PERFORMANCE CREDITS:

BENJAMIN POWELL: Adam Apocalypse. *Lord of Mad Meanings.*

ROY SCINTEI: Edward Cross. *Skull and Bones.*

SONIA KURACH: Elliot Hornell. *Sanity made sane.* Co-Author of 'Tales from The Animated Assembly Vol.1'.

ALEX REIN: Issac Hornell. *Throne of a Thousand Thieves.*

JOSEPH DAWSON: Godfear. *Light of a Lie.*

SARA ALVES: World Painter. *Ensemble of a Thousand Faces.*

ELENA DUBENKO: World Painter. *Ensemble of a Thousand Faces.*

ANNA HOWARTH: World Painter. *Ensemble of a Thousand Faces.*

THOMAS GREENFIELD: The voiceover of Colin Peterson.

THE SYMPHONY OF ADAM APOCALYPSE

Written by

Joseph Dawson

PERFORMANCE STRUCTURE:
This work should be performed in one of the following prescribed formats, alternative arrangements of scenes from The Symphony may only be performed with express permission of Animated Assembly Theatre Company Ltd. For this and all other enquiries related to 'The Symphony of Adam Apocalypse' please contact us using the email below.

Company Email:
AnimatedAssemblyTheatreCompany@gmail.com

FORMAT ONE: COMPLETE NARRATIVE
Movement I, Movement II, Movement III (Both Chapters)

FORMAT TWO: DUAL NARRATIVE
Movement I and Movement II or
Movement III (Both chapters)

FORMAT THREE: SINGLE NARRATIVE
Movement I or
Movement II or
Movement III (Chapter I only)

NOTES ON MOVEMENT I

Intended Performance Style: Expressionistic. Physical. Performative. Loud. Animated. Emotive.

Intended Mise-En-Scene: Noir. Decadent. Psychological. Personification. Visceral. Vile.

Movement I of The Symphony tells the story of 'The Everyman Family' On the surface, from the perspective of a down on his luck and heavily dissolutioned failed artist and father 'Edward Everyman' Whereas in actuality, the narrative as we encounter it through the performance, is told from the perspective of the child, 'Adam' who, in this nightmarish fantasy, is forced to live out a heavily condensed, radical experience of his childhood.

Fragmented memories, vicious roleplays and psychological trauma all play out here. The nature of everyone's actions within the movement stem from Adam's own recollection and interpretation of all that he witnessed as a boy. In essence, Movement I tells the story of two narratives, the genuine disillusionment and fall of the father, and the legacy of those events as recalled by the child. There is room for debate concerning whether or not 'Colin' and 'Brian' are actually genuine radio presenters, or merely personifications of a conflict within Edward's or Adam's mind.

When Adam ceases to portray the role of his father for brief parts of the work, there are subtle contradictions in his language and reasoning for his fall into madness, even his feelings towards his mother radically shift from line to line. Therefore, labelling Adam as an 'unreliable narrator' and calling into question the wild strangeness about the behaviour of our characters, which prompts an assumption that everybody merely exists as a personification of Adam's emotional connection to a specific fact of his childhood.

Within the first issue of work, during Edward's supposed exchange with the priest, whereby, in truth, Adam consciously accepts the mantle of his father's role in the coming story. We also happen to learn of Adam's true whereabouts through several pieces of information. His irritation at the utterance of the word "Case." And his remark "The preacher does take many forms." Implies his fate which comes to pass in Movement II. The setting of Chicago during the second world war, in a poor district of the city named "The Noir." is not a literal representation of time and setting, rather it engages with the stereotypical nostalgic, noir coat setting. A time where movies were better, society was kinder, and children didn't obsess over television.

In reality, this movement is set in 2044, during the second invasion of Vietnam by The United States, as tensions between China rise to an all-time high following their annexation of Myanmar. The first battle of the war imitates many features of the infamous D-Day Invasion, with South Korea serving as an invasion staging area, as The United Kingdom once did. Meanwhile, due to an oppressive trade war between superpowers, economic devastation is rife, and an everyday family, falls apart in its wake, the child of which, as is implied, will become a dangerous idealist in the wake of his father, akin, in some respects to Adolf Hitler.

CHARACTERS

EDWARD: A middle-aged man, already too far gone.

ELLEN: A dissatisfied middle-aged woman, vindictive beneath the surface.

FATHER: A late twenties, local priest, the epitome of the falseness within the church.

BOSS: A middle aged capitalist slob, more concerned about meeting quotas than human decency.

COLIN: An intellectual, a man who accepts and settles with the 'facts'

BRIAN: A radical man of conjecture and chaos.

THE SYMPHONY OF ADAM APOCALYPSE

MOVEMENT ONE

'Birth'

MOVEMENT I ISSUE I

'Dystopia of Discontent'

What appears to be 1940's Chicago. The land of the American dream? The working-class district of 'The Noir' A ruined church. EDWARD sits, smoking in the middle of the floor, beneath a white stark light, a ray of hope. It's far too late for that. He looks up, his pale and sickly complexion is a disturbing sight. He is interrupted by a projection of the Second World War, various images of fighting, images of The Great Depression's impact upon America. The sound of radio crackle. We hear a brief conversation between COLIN, an intellectual representative of 'The System' and BRIAN, an associate of a different kind of chaos.

COLIN: We interrupt this regularly scheduled programme to bring you a piece of breaking news, we are receiving unconfirmed reports that as of 06:30am European Central Time, The Allied Forces have invaded the North-West region of Normandy, France. While some broadcasters have questioned the validity of this information, in light of the fact that no German newspapers seem to have reported on the invasion.

A well trusted source stationed in Upottery, England, has personally verified that at an undefined time, Douglas C-47 aircraft, filled with parachute infantryman, departed the airfield there en masse, with the intention to arrive in the region on a critical secret mission prior the invasion itself. Brian, there's a ton of information there…what do you make of all this?

BRIAN: I'd hardly be surprised, Colin. A battle can often be decided before even a single shot is fired. You know, I wonder if when all is said and done, and the battlefields fall silent once again. Which they will. Will we finally take the necessary actions to prevent anything like this happening again?

COLIN: What we must remember is that The Great War's influence on the current calamity is overwhelming, had there not been-

BRIAN: Let me stop you right there, if you're going to tell me, "one war inevitably indemnifies the next." Then you condemn the world to fire and ruin, and I will be forced to throw my shoe at you, Colin. If that is your stance, then why stop there? A Great Depression has ravaged this country to the bones, should the people ravage back, what then? Nothing would be left. I pray, Colin, that we learn from this war, even if it to be just a small ounce of humility.

BRIAN: You need only look at the world around you today, with all of these merchants of death towering over us, even in our own homes, going by their many names and reasons. No-one has ever had more reason than they have had in this moment to ask, "What is one man capable of?" And believe me, it is a dangerous question to ask.

...Let us pray that your belief in our system, even in its self-assured arrogance, does not render one who might have an answer, for God help anyone who should stand in his way.

The radio dies.

FATHER enters, a clean-cut priest, he views Edward as one would look at shit upon the end of their shoe. Get off! Damn you. Get off!

21

FATHER: I didn't see you come in.

EDWARD: No? Maybe I didn't want you to see me come in. People do like surprises sometimes, wouldn't you agree, Father?

FATHER: …Depends on the surprise, I suppose. In your case-

EDWARD: *(Wincing)* My **case**?

FATHER: You don't like that word?

EDWARD: If you eat soup three times a week, more likely than not, you don't order it at a restaurant.

EDWARD glares at FATHER, who quickly moves the conversation along.

FATHER: In our…situation, then. It's good to see you. I wished you had called, though. I can't stay long, perhaps we should do this another time?

EDWARD: *(Curious)* You're always so busy these days, with your schedule, it's a wonder how you have time for anything else. Even God rested on the seventh day, Father, what did you do?

FATHER: I prayed.

EDWARD: *(Scoffing)* Of course.

Beat.

FATHER: Now that we've gone through the usual trivialities, straight to the point. Do you have something you want to tell me, Edward?

EDWARD: When it's not me who wants to talk about it, I don't see why I should do it for other people.

FATHER: That's what I figured you'd say. Has it ever occurred to you, coming here, talking to me-

EDWARD: We are talking.

An uneasy silence in a holy place.

FATHER: Has it ever occurred to you, talking about particular things, it might bring you...some sense of peace?

EDWARD: I don't give a shit about peace; don't you listen to the news? It's too late for peace.

FATHER: Is it?

EDWARD: Depends on what you want to hear.

FATHER: I can only help you if you let me.

EDWARD: Am I not letting you, Father? Or have you not given me reason to let you?

FATHER: You're here, I'm glad. I just wish you'd brought your troubles with you.

EDWARD: I've been here many times, Father. Here and not here, down the barrel of a gun. I did not forget my troubles as much as I have lost interest in handing them to people like you.

Beat.

FATHER: Why?

EDWARD: Because it never accomplishes a goddamn thing.

FATHER engages in hypocrisy, sighing over Edward for his sins in this place.

EDWARD: You want to hear an analogy that might have some truth to it? Seems relevant...given the circumstances.

FATHER: Sure.

EDWARD: Of course you do, I mean, that's what the bible is all about, right? Moral analogies, don't shit on God's hand or else he'll swarm you with flies and fever, right?

Beat.

FATHER: You were saying there was an analogy? Or would you rather us engage in another debate about the merits of religion?

EDWARD: I'll take the first option, considering you'd lose the second.

FATHER: I could walk away.

EDWARD: If you were going to, you'd have done it already.

A standoff, FATHER blinks first.

Right, so, here goes, a couple of years ago, there's this kid out in... somewhere like Chicago, poor, dangerous, why not? Could be anywhere, but who really gives a fuck? His father is a drunk piece of shit who's saying whatever he's gonna say, a real loser, who's given up on life. His mother...he thinks she's broken a little, he blames his father.

EDWARD: Anyway, she ends up dying somehow, maybe she kills herself, maybe she just slashes her fucking wrists and dies in a fucked-up way. Father, he's too drunk to fucking do anything, the kid, he shows up a few hours after she's bled so much, the Nile's having a communist inspired nostalgia trip, you know what I mean? She's been there a while, a real long while. The kid, she sent him out for fish…or to his room for something stupid, no it was the fish, it's better that way. See, because she was clever enough to know how long it would take for him to walk to Monroe Street and back again, ah well…she can't have been that fucking clever, she's dead.

Anyway, this kid, he's back home, he puts the fish supper down, calling out, stumbles over the old drunk guy called a father, he's so done with that prick, he just walks on past, doesn't even stare at him and feel disappointed anymore. So, the kid, what the fuck is the kid doing? He puts the fish down, he doesn't know how to cook it, I mean, he can do a lot of shit, a lot more than most kids can do, but, of course, he's a kid, and what does a kid always do when their asshole father is too drunk to fucking pull his weight?

FATHER: He looks for his mother?

EDWARD: *(Quickly)* Fucking A', he looks for his fucking mother, right. So, he finds the bathroom, door open just slightly, how the fuck did it open like that when she's in the bath? I don't know, maybe the devil came in and did it, I really don't know. Anyway, here's what happens, the kid pushes on the door, slow creak…you know the sound. He sees her, stops. Frozen in one place, maybe he pisses himself a little?

EDWARD takes a big sniff of the air.

EDWARD: Yep, that's it alright. He's a kid, like I said. All he can see is what's in his eyes years later, no matter how many times he sleeps, he lives it over and over, all the little pieces that put her in that bathtub. Maybe he finds a gun, or something to that effect, maybe she tells him to do it…maybe his father showed him how…he unloads three rounds right through her torso, she's sloshing around, even more blood, and, because this is a good neighbourhood, believe it or not, the kid is smart enough to know someone else heard that, but not that fucking smart or else he'd have known they were having pork chops that night, not fish. It was a Friday after all, CHRIST, doesn't anyone listen anymore?

Anyway, he's still angry, so he fires another two shots right in her fucking face, one smashes through her teeth, shame, she had a fuckable face, at least that's what the perverted old clergyman used to say in the back alley behind the 116 club as he snorted crack off the edge of a bowie knife, maybe I made that up, who knows?

The 116 Guy sounds like a piece of shit though, wouldn't you agree? Even though everybody liked him, it's not impossible, hell, you can be stood two metres away from a saint, but if you know what he did, he's a crack snorting two faced liar, that's all he was to the kid, the father too I think. As for the other shot, lodged in the head, nothing exciting. He marches downstairs and fires off the last bullet. But he doesn't kill the abusive piece of shit, our father, God in the old chair, oh no, he just wanders on by him like he had a hundred times before, no…he shoots the fish. Why the hell would he do that? Shoot the fucking fish? I couldn't figure it out, till I did.

EDWARD: We don't destroy things that exist as we expect them to be. We destroy the things that don't. The things that surprise us. Somewhere between the cradle and the grave, everyone desires to kill Santa Claus. If the father had moved out the chair, he'd have died. If he pleaded, he'd have died. But no, he sat there, as he was supposed to...and she was supposed to get her head smashed in every night by the old man, the boy was supposed to cry, but he survived, he was clever, he had the gun, and everybody feared him and tore at him... and that fish was supposed to get cooked, that's why he did it.

...Because he did know, they were supposed to have pork chops that night. The fish should've never been there to begin with. Is it just me, or does all that make perfect sense?

FATHER: In this analogy...what happened to the boy?

EDWARD: Life.

Beat.

FATHER: How have you been sleeping lately?

EDWARD: Just fine. This city has gone half to shit, between that...my fucking rent climbing through the roof, my dead-end job and my dead-end life, I'm starting to wish I was that fish. I'd pay top dollar if I could take all the horseshit in my head and just blow it out the water somehow. That's wishful thinking for you. Fishful thinking...that's a good one. I like to do that sometimes, make myself laugh. I've been told I have an ironic sense of humour, what about you, father? Do you laugh?

FATHER: Sure.

EDWARD: A shame you don't like puppets, you'd be in for a hell of a show down at the 'J.R Havana', then again, I don't know how you'd feel about Cabaret, at least below your pants line.

FATHER: How is the puppetry going?

EDWARD: Ventriloquism.

FATHER: Right, sorry.

EDWARD: Don't be, I didn't know the difference either, once.

Beat.

FATHER: Things will turn around.

EDWARD: Well, see that's the problem. They already did. You see, people are…funny little things. You give half of the people out there what they want, the other half will burn every building in a hundred miles of anywhere. Somebody got what they wanted, for me to lose everything I had. When you're staring someone like that in the face, someone who's responsible. Do you want to know what I'd like to do?

FATHER: What?

EDWARD: I'd like to be less polite than common decency compels me to be.

Beat.

I'm sorry, Father. I didn't mean to talk like that. It's just…it feels like the whole world has just gone…rotten. And, I almost want to see it snap…just a little bit. I don't think that's unreasonable.

EDWARD: To stop going around on this hamster reel from day to day. You think it's so crazy to admit that's how I feel? …I'm gonna be late for dinner, I don't think you're coming, are you? No? Alright then.

FATHER: Well, let's make sure we do this again.

EDWARD: …The preacher does take many forms doesn't he, Father?

EDWARD exits. FATHER's attentive and compassionate gaze turns malevolent, he too, exits.

END OF ISSUE I

'The Happiest Family in The World'

The radio returns.

COLIN: In every story you ever heard, there is always a duality, between the facts and those who interpret them. We are often told "Seeing is believing." Yet, through whose eyes is such a bold statement so pure? Most of us might see the world in the same light, the same details, a door is where a door is, a church is where a church is. But if I were to ask you where was hope, where was right or wrong, or mercy, there is no map leading to all mankind's hopes and prayers.

BRIAN: Good.

COLIN: Good?

BRIAN: If, such a thing existed, it wouldn't matter if every hope and prayer, enough for every man, woman and child lay in some huge pot of gold at the end of the rainbow. There are two things I can promise you that'll happen. Someone will want to get there first, and someone will want to open a damn toll booth.

The radio dies. An apartment on Delrow Street, beneath a stark light, lays a plain dinner table. At one end, EDWARD, incredibly unenthused, scooping the watery soup around before him with a silver spoon. On the opposite side, ELLEN, an overly positive housewife with a painfully large smile. Between them, a red balloon, tied to the chair with a piece of thin string, a sad face drawn on its skin. The child. You can cut the tension with a knife. ELLEN is patronising in her sweet kindness, EDWARD is bitter as hell, he'll call it all out one of these days, she doesn't need to.

30

ELLEN: How was work, dear?

EDWARD: …Fine.

ELLEN: How was church, dear?

EDWARD: …Fine.

ELLEN: How is dinner, dear?

EDWARD: …Fine.

ELLEN: How are you, dear?

Beat.

EDWARD: Fine.

ELLEN: That's good…I'm glad to hear it. I know you've been so terribly busy lately, I just wanted to make sure you were alright. It would really bother me, you know. If you weren't.

EDWARD: …That's very kind of you.

ELLEN: It's very important to me, you know, that you're alright.

EDWARD: …Likewise.

Silence.

ELLEN: *(To the balloon)* Adam, aren't you going to tell your father your big news? I've been so excited about it; I haven't known what to do with myself all day.

EDWARD looks towards the balloon, as if he knows how ridiculous this situation is.

EDWARD: ...Well?

The Balloon, of course, says nothing.

EDWARD's gaze shifts between the balloon and ELLEN.

ELLEN: ...He's just shy. He did well in school today, he's going to be playing the flute.

EDWARD: The flute? Well, that's...musical? When did he pick that up?

ELLEN: I was telling Adam about how I wanted to be a musician, do you remember what I was like when we first met? Always dreaming and scheming, so many stories, eh? I hear they're offering scholarships at particular schools for...particular families. Might be worth a look?

Silence.

EDWARD: Sure. What's one more bill?

ELLEN: Now, who's a grumpy Gustavo, eh? Don't listen to him, Adam, daddy is very proud of you. We are a very creative family, aren't we? Musicians and Ventriloquists, perhaps we have an opera singer or two? Who knows?

EDWARD: I know I don't.

ELLEN: My uncle Kurt, he played the saxophone.

EDWARD: Good for him.

ELLEN: It sure was! He met a few musicians down South, toured the whole country with his jazz fuelled touring band. Had this buddy of his that he used to rave about, oh you should've seen them together...

ELLEN: ...They were begging them to up and dance an improv or two at every Jazz club from New York City to Paris, a shame about them losing their shirts as they did, still. It happens I suppose, right? Can't sustain a career on a hobby...or a family.

Silence.

EDWARD: That's why I work a dead-end job.

ELLEN: And I am so proud of you, really, I am. I mean, how could I not be?

EDWARD: Who knows?

Beat.

ELLEN: How was your show the other night?

EDWARD: It was...passable. Just, need a new act. People are getting tired of the previous iterations of the character.

ELLEN: How do you mean?

EDWARD: Well, Adam 'The Kind' was too optimistic, came across more annoying than anything else. Too high pitched, too forgiving, my mistake, nothing that people hate more than to see someone who doesn't fall to everybody else's' level. Even though everybody else would hang the equal level for their own victory if they could, everybody wants to be a king.

EDWARD: Adam 'The Entertainer' he was supposed to be charismatic, more in touch with everyone. I pictured a guy as smooth as they came, just wasn't interesting enough, in a room of fat cats, the entertainer isn't anything but a pussy.

ELLEN: Edward.

(Indicating the balloon).

EDWARD: Oh, I'm sorry, you're right, I mustn't tell the truth to such a young child, I would hate for him not to grow up, SURPRISED, about how cruel the real world is, you're totally right. That was the third iteration, you know, Adam 'The Honest' He was supposed to be a tongue and cheek commentator, they tore him apart, it's as my old man used to say… "Never show an ugly woman the mirror, or an overconfident man, a measuring tape." It's all about struggle I guess, but it's fine, because I can thank God, I have such a wonderful family…can't I honey? I'm sorry, I suppose I'm just a little tired.

ELLEN: I understand.

EDWARD: You do?

ELLEN: Oh, I surely do…I was just saying to Nancy the other day, my shoes were hurting something awful, I couldn't understand why. I mean, I've had these shoes for so many years, and they've always been so comfortable. So, I told Nancy, "I don't get it, why are these shoes hurting so much?" And Nancy said, "It's not your shoes, Ellen, no, it's your damn feet." And I laughed "Oh Nancy, you're so right, I've been wearing these shoes too much, I need to rest my feet from these shoes, but I wouldn't want to do that in person, it's not proper behaviour for a woman to not wear her shoes at the office."

34

ELLEN: So, I thought "Whatever will I do?" And that's when it hit me, "I should be able to take my shoes off at home!", so sometimes, I will. And that's how the whole problem took care of itself, and I was so darn happy, I could hardly believe it.

Silence, what did we just hear?

EDWARD: ...Yeah, you're right, that's the exact same thing...thank you.

EDWARD stands up.

ELLEN: Aren't you going to finish your dinner?

EDWARD: *(Furiously calm)* ...I'm not hungry.

ELLEN: How are those shoes I got for you, honey? I wouldn't want them to become uncomfortable.

Beat.

EDWARD: ...Don't worry about it.

END OF ISSUE II

MOVEMENT I ISSUE III

'Reflections of Heritage'

The radio returns.

BRIAN: It is a profound tragedy, that so many children must remember their childhoods through their father's eyes. Our parents serve us with a living and breathing anthology of parables told in our time. A pity, that pearls that once shined so bright, seem now so tarnished, when exposed in a truthful light.

The radio dies.

Edward's studio, the apartment. EDWARD enters with a blank faced, child sized doll, he sets upon a table. Watching him, the balloon.

EDWARD: You wanted to watch, so eager. Tell me, what did you expect to see? A marvel of a man, a prodigy of his time...or a fool, nothing more than a stumbling drunk. I'm sorry to disappoint you. Then again, I suppose we've disappointed each other, haven't we? All these years. Me doing what I could to make ends meet, while you watched, helplessly. Your mother told me you'd been using my name, what's the matter...isn't "Adam." Worthy enough for you? Hmm?

EDWARD: Doesn't it sing your glory to the masses!? Let me save you time, there is no glory, there is nothing to praise, out there, with them...there's nothing other than dust, and grime and darkness. That's the way the world really is...the way I see it. There's one piece of advice I can give you about the world out there; Never show an ugly woman the mirror, or an overconfident man a measuring tape.

EDWARD approaches the balloon.

36

EDWARD: Why are you crying? Do you think that'll save you? Or stop them? You can cry for the rest of your life, and they'll do nothing but call you a "Sad man." Let me tell you something, son, staying silent doesn't scare away all the monsters. There are those that will find you, and rip you, and burn you, the more you stay silent, the more you try to think of others...the less you'll want to live. And until you can understand that, you are not worthy of my name. You know how proud I'd have been to be able to call you my son? Instead of naming you after me, I named you after this...

EDWARD approaches the puppet, making the puppet cover its eyes.

A frail, pathetic, deluded, disappointment. But, 'innocent' Just as you are. Perhaps I'd respect you if you were a little less "innocent." Perhaps you'd respect me...huh, never thought of it that way. Maybe that's it, we've tried everything else...maybe, Adam 'The Truthful' Oh no, far too preachy.

I know, there was Adam 'The Ironic' but, irony isn't fun when it's irony alone. Perhaps, that's been my fatal flaw, my misstep in this dance, trying to tell the world how it sees itself, when I think how it sees itself is wrong. So, I'll show them my world, make them live through it, endure it. However I can. But maybe a drink first, after all, for someone to break free of mind control, a little inebriation is half the battle.

END OF ISSUE III

MOVEMENT I ISSUE IV

'Pride of Work'

A factory floor, EDWARD stands lifeless, he guzzles from a pocket flask. The BOSS enters, a large man with greasy, unkept, features. A stained white shirt, and ragged tie, the epitome of low-level management. He speaks quickly, never listening, just waiting to talk some more.

BOSS: Edward!

EDWARD: Yes?

BOSS: Are you well?

EDWARD: Yes.

BOSS: Is work going well?

EDWARD: Yes.

BOSS: How's the wife?

EDWARD: Yes.

BOSS: That bad, huh? Well I'm sorry to hear about that. That really is a shame, my wife, she just returned from Paris, the other day, I haven't had a moment of rest. I said "Fine, fine, we'll take the week away somewhere."

BOSS: But then there's the choice of which cabin to stay at, fishing or hiking...planning time off is a lot of work, don't you think?

EDWARD: I can only imagine.

BOSS: Yes, I'm sure. Anyway, did you hear about the situation with the thief?

EDWARD: No, I hadn't.

BOSS: Well, someone's been pulling stock out of the arts and crafts store. A terrible world, isn't it?

EDWARD: You would know, I'm just glad you decided to tell me.

BOSS: Oh, well, you're welcome... I feel sorry for whoever's on the take, probably some really poor and desperate madman, some cutthroat, some uncultured swine...a complete state dissident.

EDWARD: Sure thing.

BOSS: They don't want to engage with people they deem more successful than them. They can't stand it, so they punish people for the sacrifices they're not willing to make. It's madness.

EDWARD: Well, that's how people work.

Beat.

BOSS: Hmm, yes...If you hear anything, do let me know.

EDWARD: Thank you.

BOSS: What's your extracurricular hobby again?

EDWARD: Working here?

BOSS: Very funny, no, I mean...you make puppets, don't you?

EDWARD: Yes.

BOSS: …That must be…creative.

EDWARD: Depends on who's making the damn things.

BOSS: Ah! Good one. You know, it's great that you're just one of those guys who doesn't need any passion in their lives, a big dream. No, you understand there's work to be done, and you'll spend the rest of your life working for someone else, and I admire that so much…I mean, yeah, you get the nice car, the nice house, all the money…but what's all that when you can't feel liberated by a hard day's work without much reward? It's like charity. In a way.

EDWARD: Pays the same, yeah.

BOSS: I look up to you, Edward. Anyway, some good news for you, I need you to work a little extra this week.

EDWARD: How on earth is that "good news." ?

BOSS: You told me you were having troubles with the wife.

EDWARD: Did I?

BOSS: Yes, so think of this as a chance to break free. Also, me and the wife…well, if you need someone to watch over the kids, you know, to give them a more…stable environment. Well, I'd be happy to do that, Eddie, ok? I'm not saying I have to, but if it's a calm, welcoming, wholesome atmosphere that they need, I will be that guy, Eddie. You hear me?

EDWARD: You're too kind. Even Christ has got nothing on you.

BOSS: Ha! Don't sweat it.

BOSS exits.

EDWARD: …Ought to bound you to a fucking cross and bleed you out, you fat pig.

The radio returns.

BRIAN: I heard, through my sources, that chimpanzees will patrol the outskirts of their territory.

COLIN: The same is true for wolves, bears, even particular species of bird. What of it?

BRIAN: Earlier, I was pondering our discussion. It got me thinking, could nationalism, of course, not cultivated as it has been through language and ritualistic tradition, be in itself, a woven flaw into our own making. Imagine, nature having her own kill switch to keep us in check, so that should we ever step out of line, or become too powerful for the Earth, we might destroy ourselves. Restoring a natural order to humanity's place in the world.

COLIN: The greatest offensive in military history is happening as we sit here, and you want to talk about nonsense?

BRIAN: I fear if we don't someday soon, the greatest offensive may be yet to come.

END OF ISSUE IV

MOVEMENT I ISSUE V

'Something Terrible'

The church. EDWARD finds himself on the floor, wrapped up in his own thoughts, smoking. FATHER stands over him once more.

FATHER: I didn't expect to see you again so soon.

EDWARD: Have you ever done something terrible, Father?

Beat.

Have you ever sinned?

FATHER: I don't know any man who hasn't.

EDWARD: Lately, I've been thinking about some terrible things. I think my wife is cheating on me.

Beat.

In fact, I know she is, but I have to pretend, don't I? When you know where you're going, there's only one way to the end. It would be nice, if things didn't turn out like they already did, don't you think?

FATHER: What do you mean?

EDWARD: If you knew something, Father. If you knew something terrible was going to happen, something which you could see the wrong in, but also something that was unavoidable, utterly. What would you do?

FATHER: I would do everything in my power to try and avoid… whatever we're talking about.

EDWARD: Oh, I know you would. But that's what they do to you in this fucking world, Father. They take your power, and then they burn you anyway.

Beat.

FATHER: I don't follow.

EDWARD: Your profession says otherwise. The point is, what if I told you I was going to…put on an act? Something years in the making, yet to everyone's eyes, it'll appear as if in no time at all, I jumped into dangerous territory without a second thought. You see, if tomorrow I take a knife and kill a few old friends, people who tormented me in my youth, the whole world would cry "Foul!" Wouldn't they? No remorse, no empathy, not even pity, no…just "Burn in hell, you son of a bitch!" That's all I'd be worth.

FATHER: I think it depends.

EDWARD: On what?

FATHER: Whether you showed remorse or empathy to them.

EDWARD: …They didn't.

EDWARD stands.

It's going to be a spectacular show, Father. I'd hate for you to miss it.

END OF ISSUE V

'Birth of Apocalypse'

EDWARD enters with the puppet, and a small tin of paint, with a fine brush. As our radio presenters return, EDWARD paints a sad face with black dot eyes, then satisfied with the puppet, he covers his eyes as he once did with the puppet, beginning to paint his own face in a similar fashion before a lonely mirror. An escalating instrumental scores our scene, the magnificence of the birth of an idea. The projection of images of various infamous and influential men from across history are placed on top of the action. The balloon child held in the hand of a terrified ELLEN, who watches from afar.

COLIN: Birth, Hope, Responsibility, Regret...tell me, what is one man capable of?

Silence. The instrumental score has its time, rising, slowly, consuming the space, bold and burning bright.

BRIAN: *(Slowly)* An idea. For all the sum of mankind's brilliance, its technological arrogance, its industrial fury...if our history has taught us anything, it is that one man with an idea, may change the world more than the world may ever have changed him.

EDWARD finds his courage in the mirror, beholding a sense of comfort and dangerous confidence, he mimics strangling a human being, the actor plays as he will.

BRIAN: For all the men who have given their lives, willingly or otherwise to a broken system...sometimes, unintentionally. As is the will of nature. A man may rise from the ashes anew, and behold the world's rawness, an otherwise unbearable truth to the many.

COLIN: What would a man like that do with that kind of…burden? How could he survive?

BRIAN: *(Slowly)* He couldn't, and so he will burn us, he will bring destruction and change to the world, an apocalypse of the old, through salvation of the new. Then, this first of us, this Adam of our Apocalypse, will serenade us to our sleep, till his world becomes ours.

The radio dies.

The instrumental score finishes, EDWARD beholds his image in the mirror with his puppet, ELLEN sets the dinner table for the following scene, still frightened. The puppet is stashed beneath the table.

END OF ISSUE VI

MOVEMENT I ISSUE VII

'The Wife'

A silent dinner, ELLEN looks away as EDWARD smiles at her, irritatingly so.

ELLEN: How was your day, dear?

EDWARD: Wonderful honey, how was yours?

ELLEN: It was...good, thank you, darling.

EDWARD: Well, I sure am glad.

ELLEN: ...You are?

EDWARD: Of course, I am so glad, God help you if I showed you how glad I was, it might...

EDWARD slams his hands on the table.

...PISS. YOU. OFF!

Silence.

ELLEN: There's something different about you today.

EDWARD: Really? You noticed. What could it be? Oh, new shoes. My shoes, comfortable, clean, roomy.

ELLEN looks beneath the table; he's still wearing the same shoes.

ELLEN: Those look like the shoes I got you.

EDWARD: Well, maybe something looks like one thing, when really, it's something else. A happy marriage, a whore wife...that's a good example, you know, affairs are fun, well, you would know.

ELLEN's reaction turns bitter, we see a foul face.

ELLEN: Ok then, let's have it out.

EDWARD: You wouldn't want that.

ELLEN: Oh, I think I would.

EDWARD: Well, I know you like a little bit of rough confession, don't you, honey?

ELLEN: I prefer it to living with a dead-end piece of shit like you.

EDWARD: Yet, you made dinner.

ELLEN: Someone has to.

EDWARD: Oh, someone will. It's a sad way to go out, this, because it's the last fucking dinner you make in this house. I want you out, I want you...GONE! You understand me?

ELLEN: That won't be a problem, the new look suits you, about the only interesting thing you've done in fifteen years.

EDWARD: Oh, you like it? It's part of my new act. Would you like to see it? I'll show you, it's...well, it's the new me. Maybe you'll like it, I sure do.

EDWARD places the puppet on his hand, he begins to test a series of voices, before finding one he enjoys, when speaking as the puppet, EDWARD's lines are referenced as 'Adam's'

ADAM: Hello, Ellen, darling, how are you today?

Silence.

EDWARD: Say hello.

ELLEN: Hello.

ADAM: Well Hi! How about a little dosage of the truth…a little secret, do you like secrets, why of course you do! You keep so many of them from your husband, and you've always thought that he didn't notice. Well, here's the secret, he did notice! He noticed when you said you didn't believe in him, time and time again, I bet you sure feel silly now, right?

ELLEN: Edward, stop it.

ADAM: Edward is unavailable at the moment; would you like to leave a message? You know how every time you ask him how his day was? Not really giving a shit about the answer, I mean, why do people do that? Ask how the other person is, and expect them to say "Ok." or it gets awkward, Jesus Christ, some people, eh? Here's the secret. It really, really pisses him the hell off when you sit there with that stupid fucking face, that should be cut up into little…PIECES…talking out of that stupid whore mouth of yours, asking him how he is when you're the worst thing about my day. And it makes him wonder. "Why don't you shut the fuck up for one day?" Huh? Why don't you just close your fucking mouth for once…always yapping in his fucking ear…

ELLEN: Honey, enough.

ADAM: Every day, he works, to come back to a son who won't talk to him...a wife...who won't fuck him...a shithole apartment, a shit job...a shit fucking life. And all he's asked for...is that you leave him alone to do what he does...which is art...far more than you or your little friends are capable of, you and Nancy...and whoever the shit hell else...are only good at one thing...spreading your fucking legs on street corners...at least I assume they're good at it, you can't be very good...because we've got not a dime or a dollar. And you have to fuck the priest, well, better than you than some ten-year-old boy, right!? Ain't that the punch?

Silence.

ELLEN throws the table over, EDWARD discards the puppet, they wrestle, the next section of this issue is a confrontation, a dance, they dig at one another, physically, verbally, the performers should be exhausted come the end of this issue.

EDWARD: That's more like it! Come on, why don't you just fucking hit me?

ELLEN: Fuck you, get the hell out of my face.

EDWARD: Oh, come on, whore, you can do better than that, what else have you fucking got? Where's that inner vindictive bitch that I know and love, let's get her in the arena...we've all got a dark side, a demon in the closet...I want to see yours with my own fucking eyes, come on.

ELLEN: You don't want to push me, it's not my fault everything in your life isn't worth two shits. You don't want to upset me.

EDWARD: Oh…you shouldn't have enticed me like that baby, all I want to do now is upset you…oh that's fun. Maybe I drink some more, see how fast I can rearrange your face with a knife, that sounds like fun, don't you think? Is that original!? Is that what you want!? Someone with interesting things to say, IS THAT WHAT **HE** DOES!?

ELLEN: You alcoholic piece of shit, you want to know why I did it? Because I couldn't stand being married to a self-loathing prick, a pathetic son of a bitch, like you. Of course, I needed to fuck my way out of this house. Hell knows there isn't any other way out of this shit hole.

EDWARD: Oh, yeah…fucking go for the jugular, right in front of the boy, slit my throat, cut my fucking eyes out for wronging you, come on, baby, come on…do it! Do it!

ELLEN: I'll fucking…I'll…You know I'll…

EDWARD: WHAT ARE YOU GONNA DO!? HUH!?

DO SOMETHING, BITCH! BESIDES RUNNING YOUR FUCKING MOUTH, DAY IN, DAY OUT…I DON'T GIVE A SHIT ABOUT WHAT ANY OF YOU HAVE TO SAY….

WHOO! OH MAN I'M ALIVE, I'M DANCING, I'M LIVING…I COULD DO THIS ALL FUCKING DAY! WHOOO!

Silence.

ELLEN: You stumble around…pretending you're something that you're not…the only fucking reason that you play with your toys like a child, is because that's the only thing that you can control, because the rest of your life is so terrible, so pitiful…

50

ELLEN: It's the last attempt of a sad fucking man to feel like he matters to someone. No wonder your parents didn't love you.

Silence.

EDWARD: Beautiful. Don't talk about my parents, I might not know what to do with myself, because according to my darling wife, I can be broken by...

Slamming his hands on the table.

TEARS!?

ELLEN: Oh, I know that hurt.

EDWARD: You think? You don't know what hurt is...tell you what, I'll do you one better...

Beat.

It's all your fault.

ELLEN: *(Sarcastic)* Good job.

EDWARD: No, you know what I'm saying...

Beat.

It was your fault, I lied. Out of pity. You are a pathetic waste of a woman. If you can't even...

EDWARD looks her up and down.

EDWARD: I don't even know what you are. Some disgusting, repulsive animal, forced to sell herself at a discount price, because no man will ever love her. Face it, honey, I'm the best you ever did.

EDWARD exits. ELLEN screams like hellfire.

END OF ISSUE VI

MOVEMENT I ISSUE VIII

'The Inevitable End'

The factory, BOSS enters, looking around. There's no sign of Edward.

BOSS: Come on, Eddie, where the hell are you?

FATHER enters, flustered.

BOSS: ...Father? What are you-

FATHER: Have you seen Edward?

BOSS: No, I've not seen him all day. What's gotten you all so flustered?

FATHER: Look, Edward came to see me yesterday...I think, well, he's in a wild way. I just got back from his place, Ellen, she's...all, well, I don't think there are words. She thinks he might be looking for us, so why don't you and me head down the police station, and get this crazy son of a bitch off our backs, huh? What's your address, 116-

EDWARD enters, carrying Adam Apocalypse.

EDWARD: And stood I did, before the might of the church and the tower, although many would've stood in my place and revelled in its awesomeness, I saw nothing but discontent, for the walls were made of skin, the framework, bones. The tower was built by the hands of slaves, indemnified by the church. The two pillars of the damned, a gateway to hell itself.

Beat.

EDWARD: Gentleman...welcome to the show.

BOSS: Hi...Edward, that's...uh, a nice look you have there.

EDWARD: Oh, you think so? I wish I could say the same, perhaps you ought to have tried that, although, it's too late for that now. The man who fucked my wife, and the man who fucked me...how they run in terror in the face of a free man.

FATHER: Is that what you call this? I spoke to Ellen, she's terrified.

EDWARD: The guilty often are. You see...when I was a boy, I remember hearing about you. For so many years all I could think of is what I'd do if I was in my father's place, would I rip you, bite you, tear you limb from limb or break you.

EDWARD: Now, here I stand, face to face. People like you, take EVERYTHING! From people like me. Venomous leeches, demanding obligation for the right to live, the right to breathe...well, gentleman, today, you will oblige me. Stop me if you've heard this one before...A capitalist, a priest and a dangerous psychopath are all in the same room at the same time...who lives, who dies?

Silence.

No ideas? Nothing to say...nothing at all? My, my...you assholes really are boring, let's ask my friend here...assholes, meet Adam Apocalypse...say hi. Now, come, come, I want to show you what I can do, so...SAY IT!

FATHER: ...Hello.

BOSS: ...Hi.

ADAM: A dirty priest and a fat ass pig…oh this should be fun! How I love fun people! Who lives, who dies!? The priest gets his ass fucked in bloody, and the pig…I'd eat his tongue…I'd eat his ribs…I'd eat him and cut him and scramble him around.

Beat.

EDWARD: You fellas look nervous…Adam was only joking; do you like him? You should, what Father despises their own child? Besides God, of course.

FATHER: Edward…why don't you just-

EDWARD: I swear to Hell's wrath…do not tell me to calm down, else it be the last thing you ever fucking say.

Beat.

You couldn't just leave me alone could you? No, oh, you had to make me suffer, I could've lived a happy life, a boring life, free of pain and suffering. BUT YOU KILLED ME! Well…behold the face of death, as it stares wildly into your eyes.

Beat.

EDWARD drops the puppet, revealing a knife.

What is one man capable of? I'll show you.

EDWARD charges towards FATHER, stabbing him to death. BOSS falls, trembling as a child.

WHOO! WHERE'S YOUR GOD NOW!? HAVE HIM STRIKE ME DOWN, OR YOUR GOD IS NOT!

BOSS: Jesus Christ…Edward…what the hell are you doing!? Oh God…you killed him. You fucking killed him!

EDWARD laughs hysterically, he crawls towards BOSS, a terrifying smile on his face, sniffing the man, frightening him.

EDWARD: That's right, I stuck him real fucking good, didn't I? You want to know what I'm gonna do next? I'm gonna cut your skin off, I'm gonna bite it, even the dead parts which don't break unless I really fucking pull…then I'm gonna chop your fucking fingers off, I'm gonna chop your cock off, your balls, I'm gonna make crackling out of you, you, you… fat piece of shit. Not so tough now, huh? Not so strong…

ADAM: NOT SO STRONG NOW, LITTLE MAN TAKING EVERYTHING FROM EVERYONE…I know, let's cut him.

BOSS: What the hell are you doing, Eddie, come on, it's me…you can't kill me…come on, please, I don't want to die. I'll…give you a raise, I'll give you an office, I'll give you my office! I'll give you fucking anything!

EDWARD: You want to buy your freedom?

BOSS: Yes, Yes! Oh God, please, name it! Anything!

EDWARD: I want one of your cabins for a long weekend, call it a sabbatical. Your boat too, that will be my payment.

BOSS: …I…what?

EDWARD: You heard me.

BOSS: Sure, I'll give you the keys right now, I promise, anything else?

EDWARD: You know, they say never trust a businessman who makes promises, it used to be clear cut as a barber's shave, that is, till the day came when businessmen became elected politicians, now a leader can be businessman, and the world doesn't know what to say. Like a father, whose daughter brings home an alcoholic biker in his mid-thirties, she marries him, the father has no fucking idea what he's gonna say. No fucking clue. ...You want to know something? You want to know who stole from you?

I DID! I DID! I DID! It feels so good to say! Oh! I DID! I DID! I DID!

BOSS: Come on, Eddie, please...I'm sorry, alright, I'm sorry about your life.

EDWARD: MY LIFE!? Why is it only my life...WHEN IT'S IN EVERYONE'S GODDAMN WAY!? ...I want the boat.

BOSS: Come on, Ed.

EDWARD: Give it over.

BOSS: Here, here, take it.

The BOSS throws the keys from his pocket towards EDWARD.

Beat.

Come on, just let's be-

EDWARD: REASONABLE!? I'll give you reasonable when I cut out your innards and tie them around a Christmas tree, then I'll take your liver and fucking eat it and chew it and bite it...did you really think a boat would save you? I LIED! I'M A LIAR! A PATHETIC, DESPERATE PIECE OF SHIT, RIGHT!?

BOSS cowers.

No...I'm not gonna kill you. You spend your whole life cutting people down...always turning a blind eye. Bring a knife to the pig's throat, and it squeals more gold than a fucking leprechaun on a goddamn rainbow. Well now...God is watching, the world is watching.... Here's what you're going to do...you want to profit off the death of dreams, the death of ambition...the death of fucking living for something? You want to turn a blind eye?

EDWARD: Oh...great merchant of death, I'll make you blind!

EDWARD carves out his eyes. The BOSS screams.

EDWARD: GET YOUR FAT FUCKING ASS UP! Come on Mr. President! Mr. Merchant! King of the fucking rats and beggars! Get up!

BOSS sluggishly stands. EDWARD forces him to drag FATHER'S body away.

END OF ISSUE VIII

MOVEMENT I ISSUE IX

'Finale'

The apartment, at the dinner table, the balloon tied to one of the chairs. EDWARD enters, with the puppet.

EDWARD: I'M HOME! DARLING, HONEY, LOVE OF MY LIFE!? Where are you!?

ELLEN enters, she holds a gun in her hand.

ELLEN: Stay back!

EDWARD: What is this? Hunting for sport!?

ELLEN: Don't, please, Eddie, I'm going, ok!? I'm just gonna go.

Beat.

EDWARD: You dumb bitch. I'm gonna cut your legs off, you'll never go anywhere again. I killed your lover…I fucking killed him, I cut him up into little pieces and ate him, I cut his fucking dick off! Let's see you fuck him now, you stupid slut!

EDWARD draws his knife.

I'm gonna bleed you, real fast, like a pig, and cook you, or no…

EDWARD: I'll keep you alive, make you see things from my perspective, for the rest of your life, living as my little puppet, 'Adam The Whore' 'Adam The Amputee' …I love it.

A dance begins between ELLEN and EDWARD.

ELLEN: ...You shouldn't tempt me.

EDWARD: Oh, you said the magic word. How does it feel? Knowing there's an empty seat at the dinner table that can never be filled, that all of your friends, your family, know you're a murderer. And now, they'll know you're a whore, a liar, a venomous snake, and for whatever is coming to me, half of it will be coming to you. I'll make sure about that. They'll never find their bodies...they'll never find yours; no-one will ever know you were alive. You understand me?

EDWARD charges forward, him and ELLEN wrestle violently with the knife, they scream at one another, tearing at each other's clothes. She gains control over the weapon, shooting him in the leg. He screams.

ELLEN: ...How do you like it!? You think you're the only one who's had to struggle!? You think it's been any easier on me!? But no! You never think about me, do you? All you see is your own damn problems...didn't you ever think that I might have problems, that I might have something to say...and you say...IT'S MY FAULT!? As if I murdered her!? You don't know the pain of living through that...

ELLEN:...But you're about to.

ELLEN takes the gun and shoots his other leg, immobilising him before pulling down his trousers, she rapes him with the bloody knife. He screams, she lets up. EDWARD cowers, laughing hysterically. ELLEN moves away from EDWARD, and approaches the balloon, still and silent as ever.

ELLEN: Ssh...it's ok. Close your eyes. I won't let him hurt you...there's no need to be afraid.

EDWARD lifts the top half of his body, looking towards ELLEN.

EDWARD: Mother.

ELLEN walks away from the balloon, placing the gun down beside it, looking towards EDWARD.

ELLEN: I have to go now, sweetie. I'm sorry.

EDWARD: No, please. It doesn't have to end like this.

ELLEN: It already has.

EDWARD: I'll make them pay for this, mother, I swear to you. I'll make them all pay for what they've done!

ELLEN: Ssh, remember what I said? Close your eyes, Adam. Imagine that you could be anyone you ever wanted to be, who would you become? What would you do?

EDWARD: …What is one man capable of?

EDWARD begins to crawl towards the balloon and the gun.

No-one ever comes, my father stays in his chair…rambling, telling me stories…my mother works her fingers to the bone for us, the monsters threaten to take our house, I realise my father was right.

ELLEN: I turn on the tap, run the hot water and fill the bath.

EDWARD reaches for the gun, reluctantly pointing it towards ELLEN.

EDWARD: She sends me out for the fish, I find her in the bath, I'M SO DISAPPOINTED! She's still alive.

ELLEN: I'm sorry, son. You have to be strong now.

EDWARD: I can't do it.

ELLEN: You have to, you already have.

EDWARD: Helpless, I pull the trigger, shoot her face into pieces! MAKE HER PAY!

A gunshot, ELLEN falls, silence, EDWARD screams.

...I killed her. There's one last round in the gun...

EDWARD turns the gun on his head.

But my father is right where he's supposed to be...so I spare him. There isn't much time to lose, I cut up her body and put the parts in a bag, just like my old man taught me. I throw her in the river, her head, her arms, her torso...her legs. Every night, I dream of the days of yesterday, every night, I remember what the world made me, but when I wake...I will make the world.

EDWARD pulls the trigger, he lays still. The light slowly begins to fade, our radio presenters return.

COLIN: You can't seriously believe; the undoing of the world could possibly come from some nobody living out their lives out in the middle of nowhere. All these men we're talking about here, were just...lucky. They had their time, saw things as they did and then the circumstances were right enough to allow them to thrive. One man can't just burn the world because he wants to.

BRIAN: No, you're right. He can't. But let me ask you this, Colin, if a man can form an idea powerful enough and find the means to articulate it, to either the many, or the mad...how long do you think the danger resides in just one person?

BRIAN: A martyr might be the first to take a step into a new world, one that has no place for the one we know. But it will be the children of the martyrs that we create, who will realise the dystopian dream of their forebears. Our way of life provokes chaos in its cruelty, then allows the free speaking people of the world the opportunity to turn chaos into culture. For the father, it was ambition, for the son?

...It will be revenge.

END OF ISSUE IX

NOTES ON MOVEMENT II

Intended Performance Style: Naturalistic. Thoughtful. Attentive. Real. Genuine. Depth. Study.

Intended Mise-En-Scene: Minimalistic. Bare. Naked. Raw. Clean. OCD. Sterile.

The sensical, when doused in misery, often tends to define what is real. Descartes' wise and renowned words should perhaps be amended to reflect this notion better "I suffer, therefore I am." In this second movement, we join 'Adam Everyman' as a young man, an infamous serial killer, idolised by the curiosities of the West.

The entirety of this portion of work takes place in a single isolated room in a private medical facility full of agenda and corruption, at least according to Adam. Whether or not, he, as the unreliable narrator can be trusted, is up to the audience. They must discern truth, from lie, from contradiction. Linearity will not save anyone here.

It is immediately established in this movement, that the country of England has suffered events which rhyme with the context of that of the first movement. An economic collapse, a world engulfed by armed conflict and a socio-political fragmentation. However, as a decade has passed from 2044 (The year in which our first movement's events truly occur) we learn quickly of how things have further devolved.

Ideas have filled the air, but so too have come those with the will to execute them. A young intern at the institution 'Edward Cross' faces an arc of decay, as it relates to his status opposite Adam, whose consistent ideological assaults on the man provoke weakness, and eventually, submission.

A pivotal example of this being when Edward reveals his father's death to Adam, inviting the madman's interest and sealing his own fate. The populace of England at this time seem to be utterly dissolutioned with the governance of the state. There is no more "King and Country." Only the interests of the individual. It seems, to those with heavy influence in the ever-destabilising political climate, caution has been thrown to the wind, increasingly so, with every passing year.

A crucial part of the experience of this movement is the relationship between Edward and his perception of time. We notice that Adam states that he is a master of indoctrination, and his alleged desire is to make Edward see as he sees. Initially, our approach to time is incredibly straightforward, yet, as the narrative progresses, a seemingly endless conversation ensues which leads us to a supposed Armageddon.

Having read the work, there is an open-ended question as to whether this Armageddon is merely an indoctrination of one man, or truly the end of days. What constitutes an apocalypse to us? Must the skies burn for all, to burn for one? This is the fundamental question which follows through to 'Movement III' and the conclusion of the overall work.

CHARACTERS

ADAM: The Master. (If applicable; Played by the same actor as EDWARD in Movement I)

EDWARD: Mid-Twenties, The Puppet.

COLIN: An intellectual, a man who accepts and settles with the 'facts'.

BRIAN: A radical man of conjecture and chaos.

THE SYMPHONY OF ADAM APOCALYPSE

MOVEMENT TWO

'Hope'

MOVEMENT II ISSUE I

'Room 116'

2054, The Edmund Hill Asylum for the Criminally Insane, Hereford, England. An interview room, ADAM sits chained to the table, a deep bloody cut on the side of his head, he winces with the pain, he smokes. The entirety of this movement takes place in this isolated space. A cold stark light without an ounce of hope above. The sound of COLIN and BRIAN speaking above our scene emerges with a crackle.

COLIN: Adam Everyman, deranged psychopath or cult leader? This is 'The Madland Podcast', your hosts, Colin and Brian here, and today you're listening to us, live in Hereford this afternoon. It's been a long time since we last recorded a show here, any thoughts on this monumental occasion, Brian?

BRIAN: Yeah, a few, Colin. It's really something to believe. But, I feel like we've been overshadowed a little this morning, I don't know if you want to talk about that now, get it out of the way?

COLIN: Sure thing, for our audience, of course, as our podcast plays all around the world, it would be right to just take some time to explain a little bit about what's been going on, before we get to the incident this morning. So, Brian, tell us, who is Adam Everyman?

BRIAN: Well, he's trouble. But he isn't crazy.

66

COLIN: Here we go. The controversy.

BRIAN: I'm just saying, if you ask me, there's nothing wrong with him at all.

COLIN: Yeah, sure, I mean, he killed seven people... that we know of. One, an international heartthrob in the music business, Helena Crawford.

BRIAN: Yeah...but still, just because you brutally murder someone, or seven people in this instance. Well, it's terrible, of course, but it doesn't make them mentally ill, and I think we have to make that difference in what we're talking about here. Particularly with the name of our show, you know?

COLIN: Come on, Brian, it's textbook, there's some fucked-up upbringing, the kid grows up and has a twisted view of everything, and then decides to butcher a load of people. He's in Edmund Hill for a reason, my friend.

BRIAN: Yeah, so are the doctors.

COLIN: So, what? Killing is normal behaviour now?

BRIAN: When is anything "normal behaviour." ? If you asked me, "Is Adam Everyman crazy?" I say no.

COLIN: What's that based on?

BRIAN: Because I think he knows exactly what he's doing, and worse still, I think that's what he wants you to think. That he's bat shit crazy and we're trying to butcher what he's about because we don't understand him. Now, the bunch of freaks running around trying to copycat the man...that's fucking crazy, otherwise, Adam Everyman is as sane as I am.

COLIN: Well, we agree on that last part at least.

The radio dies.

EDWARD CROSS, a young medical intern enters, an identity tag pinned upon his chest, over his heart.

ADAM: The Pied Piper plays to Friedrich's song, still he comes, for he does not hear it.

EDWARD: I was going to start with "Good afternoon."

ADAM: Maybe I'm not having a "Good afternoon." though, I don't think you are either.

EDWARD takes a seat opposite Adam.

EDWARD: Are you sure you don't want that... *(Indicating Adam's wound)* looked at?

ADAM: I wanted to talk to you first. About a deeper wound.

EDWARD: You could've asked, did you think about that?

ADAM: *(Venomous)* I did "Ask."

EDWARD: The Nurse that's now lying in intensive care might use a different word. That is, if she is ever able to talk again.

ADAM: Not so much of a loss to the world, what's one less dry, dull, monotonous voice? You, on the other hand... You're rather confrontational for a man in your profession, a model indictment of the consequences of the privatisation of The National Health Service.

ADAM: Shouldn't you be attempting to convince your friends through the looking glass that you are a competent practitioner of societal indoctrination? Asking me why I tried to claw that young woman's tongue out, her eyes tearing up, her throat humming in fear...do my crimes anger you, Mr. Cross?

EDWARD: I do not allow them to anger me, Mr. Everyman. Nor you. I'm here to discuss your case.

ADAM: That word...the preacher does take many forms, don't you think? Mr. Cross. Since you've taken us straight to relevant business, a quality I respect, even admire. I won't insult your intelligence to ask you if you're aware of how I sustained my injury this morning?

EDWARD: I've been thoroughly informed, yes.

ADAM: So I can see. But, don't worry...We'll fix that in no time.

EDWARD: How do you mean?

ADAM: You, are wrong to think that I am the one who needs a confession between the two of us. The injury, I consider it a business expense of sorts, after all...you were the one who gave it to me.

EDWARD: I'm sorry?

ADAM: Awakening from a dream, it's mind altering, quite literally, don't you think? So, if you beat my head in, then you were the one who hurt that innocent girl too. Meaning, the crimes that anger you, are your own...tell me, do you allow **that**, Mr. Cross?

EDWARD: There are witnesses who have testified that you-

ADAM: Blind children wandering through the garden, and you hail them as navigators? I feel them, out there, gathered like rats waiting to feast upon every drop of oil that prizes itself from my lips. Championing a naïve child of an alcoholic father as their canary in the mine. Even birds are fearful of the dark, you know.

EDWARD: You think they see you as-

ADAM: I think they see nothing. And I am not their canary, Mr. Cross. Look *(Indicating his chains)* I am unable to fly. You are their champion, and they will clip your wings and torch your lungs for their agendas, their schemes, their...book deals. That's what they do. They take everything, all our power, they always do. Don't they?

Beat.

Context. I saw you yesterday. A passing encounter that I never imagined would hold any significance. You think of everyone who's ever been integral to your life, for good or bad. So easily, they could've faded by the wayside like stray trucks on a rainy road, passing with red lights in the drenched air. We never know what we've never had, because if we did, it would be soul crushing, wouldn't it? You never looked at me, but I saw your badge, your totem, your shrunken head. You never thought of the name, and I never thought of it, how could I?

You wear the name of my father... *(Almost sickly)* Edward. And, dare to stand before me as a man of ambition? Rewarded, for blind ignorance to the truth I am imprisoned for. The truth that my father suffered for...the truth that my mother suffered for. I dreamed of them...wore his fears as mine, his guilt as mine...it was hellish and strange. I was in agony, my body would not move, but, I saw...demons lurking in every corner, fragmented moments, faces upon stained glass.

70

ADAM: Etched into my mind's eye, my father's name…because of you. A passing murder of a good man, the obituary of the modern world.

EDWARD: That's…well, I'd be surprised if they didn't offer you a book deal next.

ADAM: *(Raising his hands)* What do you call this?

EDWARD: You first.

ADAM: No, you.

A showdown, silence. ADAM blinks first but tries to cover it as his own decision.

…You unsettled me, Mr. Cross. And I won't lie, I do not enjoy living in a world where a man can do such a thing. And yet, I am aware, in their eyes, I am a marvel, a wonder, a work of art, the work of indoctrination is a powerful tool. This is how I know of you. And so, our game begins, you will play their canary and I will play the dark. At my convenience. I will play with you, and you alone.

Surely a man so motivated in his career could at least imagine the desire of knowing me, the value of damned secrets. I will tell you enough to make you the wealthiest man in this place…but, you will never know wealth. For my price will be horror, brutal, unwavering and always. *(Desperate, almost wincing)* For I desire you to know the pain you inflict, Edward. The pain upon me, at each passing moment of your existence, and I too will be brutal, unwavering and always. For, if they silence me…*(venomous)* They will have to silence you…

EDWARD stands, and heads towards the door.

ADAM: Do be a friend and bring a game next time, I do so easily get bored of watching mice run wheels.

CROSS exits, ADAM remains.

END OF ISSUE I

MOVEMENT II ISSUE II

'The Symphony'

The radio returns. ADAM sits, listening to the radio presenters whenever they return, reacting as he wishes.

COLIN: I don't want the conversation to become too heavy today. I don't know, it's a tense time for all of us.

BRIAN: So, we thought we'd calm everyone down and talk about a serial killer? Well, sounds like us.

COLIN: It's a dangerous time at the moment, globally. I don't think it's ever been this bad.

BRIAN: Yes, it's very 'Cold War' isn't it?

COLIN: Not just the global situation, but even here in the UK, for those who don't know, maybe our listeners in the States, there's this radical left group in London, taking part in all the riots going on there, at first, they were just a digital outrage sensation, always stepping over the line, "Are they good? Are they not?" The usual stuff-

BRIAN: Yeah, I've heard some bad shit. It's really easy to get away with things these days if you agree with the right things publicly.

COLIN: There's always bad shit. The point is, they're seriously calling for The United Kingdom to be dissolved as a nation, the flag, the history...replaced with, I'm not making this up... "New Albion." Because apparently the UK's history is too oppressive, so it all needs to come down.

BRIAN: Well, like I said, it's not that they're fucked up in the head, or in serious need of some help or something. That's excusing them, you know? I think the people running that show know exactly what they're doing. And, I honestly think the reason we gaslight these groups and people, even this 'Cult of Adam' is because, as we've done throughout history to women when they're too powerful, science when it completely disproves religion, and God, those people are so desperate to hold on to whatever's left, even though the church is totally-

COLIN: Whoah, we're going off on a tangent here, where are we going with this?

BRIAN: We're terrified these groups might actually believe what they're saying. And once an idea's got enough steam, somebody always gets the idea to build a paid institution around it. An old friend of mine out in Hollywood, he used to say, "Religion is fine, church on the other hand…"

The radio dies. ADAM sits in his usual place, EDWARD enters with a chess board and a small box of paperwork, he sets up the game, in silence ADAM watches Edward like a hawk, you can cut the tension with a knife. As the rest of the work progresses, when appropriate, both ADAM and EDWARD make a move.

ADAM: My favourite…tell me, do you enjoy music?

Beat.

EDWARD: Who doesn't?

ADAM: I'd wager at least one poor soul; else the question would have no reason to exist. Unless the question existed for the question's own sake.

EDWARD: …Whatever you want.

ADAM eyes up Edward, a smile.

ADAM: You protested your return?

EDWARD: I did.

ADAM: Was it something I said?

Beat.

What's the matter? Cat got your tongue? Forgive me, I have my father's sense of humour, but my mother's sense of irony. What can I say? I have acquired tastes.

EDWARD: Don't we all?

ADAM: I asked myself that question every day at music school, the most revealing three years of my life, would you be interested as to know why?

EDWARD: …Sure.

ADAM: Because it taught me, as a principle lesson…that evidence of the hypocrisy of mankind is better found in the world of artists, than the terrible practices of lawyers and politicians. Even private black site medical institutions with terrible dirty secrets, abundant in stains on the carpet. You see…Robin Hood, everybody just loves him, don't they? He steals from the rich to give to the poor…right? In what world should economic status dictate the exoneration of thievery? Out there, those 'Liberals'…they think they're saving the world, calling themselves "progressive."

ADAM: It is easy to say the right things, easier still to print those words on paper. But changing the inevitably malicious nature of the human condition? That in itself…is a monumental task. Only a fool imagines a fire is doused without fury on the part of the water.

EDWARD: What does this have to do with anything?

ADAM: Oh, only everything. The obvious is forgotten by the many, till, when it is presented again, its obviousness must be ushered aside as to maintain the security of the ideological ego. They say that anything can be art, they say that. But their actions always defy their rhetoric. Artists, I mean.

EDWARD: Is this what you tell that little fan club of yours?

ADAM: It's what I'm telling you.

Beat.

EDWARD: What you just said, isn't that just the same with politicians and lawyers? How is it a better example?

ADAM: Oh yes, it's very much the same, but those professions exist as we expect them to exist, the artist struggles against what it should be. It is a fish out of water. It is that which does not exist as we expect it to, that is doomed.

EDWARD: So, what is the artist, in your mind?

ADAM: Dead. *Something that imitates life can never hope to become life, it belongs at the bottom of the ocean, sunk by the perseverant mind. an imitation of something is a shadow.*

ADAM: I presented a bold new vision of sound, nonsensical, supposedly. Yet to my ear, it was representative of the symphony of mankind, four movements, the birth of the sound, chaotic and painful, the hope of the sound, the responsibility of committing to one's own ideology and lastly...regret. No sound at all.

Beat.

They rejected my work, so I rejected theirs. The symphony of mankind became...one of my own. Yet, beyond my own name. 'The Symphony of Adam Apocalypse'. A new piece, one far bloodier in nature, and when I played...the world listened, finally.

EDWARD: Why "Adam Apocalypse."? How did you come up with the name?

ADAM: My father was a Ventriloquist, he named his acts, 'Adam The Kind' 'Adam The Cruel' everything you could imagine, then he named me, but would still not permit me my name. (*Mournful*) How I envied his love of make believe and strings.

EDWARD opens the box, revealing a handful of a child's drawings, all scenes from Movement I.

EDWARD: Do you recognise these?

Beat.

You had quite the imagination as a boy, didn't you? I assume these are drawings of your childhood?

A projection bursts to life, showing the images over the scene.

ADAM: You wouldn't believe.

EDWARD: Here, this one, that's your father, sitting in his chair, your mother...she's in the kitchen. What's with the balloon?

ADAM: You of all people should know the answer to that question.

EDWARD: I of all people?

ADAM: Enlighten me, when your father came home, drunk, lost, the fragility of the world seeped in amongst his stink. Quite naturally, I imagine, you were terrified, or did you not "Allow." Him to terrify you? Perhaps you cried to God, if that's your poison. Don't be insulted, all those who follow a God are deluded, self-righteous, sanctimonious victims of guilt and fear.

EDWARD: Well, at least we know I don't have to ask you about your religious views.

ADAM: You don't, though I am curious about yours.

EDWARD: I don't know.

ADAM: Spare me the centrist view of agnosticism. It is a middle ground reserved for those who do not wish to tell their children that Santa Claus is not worthy of war nor gold.

EDWARD: I think there might be more to it than that.

ADAM: There isn't. A book written after a man's death; monuments as sinful as the wonders of Las Vegas. Where once upon a time, priests used their influence to govern, now, they use the acquisition of money through televisions, promising fortune and favour...

ADAM: Vatican City has commanded far more murder than I have, yet here I sit, and there they stand…tearing apart families as they will.

EDWARD: If we could get back to the point?

ADAM: You know what it's like to feel helpless. So, do I. My father was a downtrodden man, who believed in the right things but was cursed by the rich and the poor, by men of ambition, men of God, men like you. My mother was…a victim of his pain. I watched helplessly, and I was helpless. To desire a legacy and be denied such a thing is a terrible fate, don't you think so? Fills you with ideas, that in itself is a legacy of its own, I suppose. It's helplessness, the feeling. Light and as silent as a balloon, is that how it felt for you? When they found my mother's body, torn into pieces, they never for one second could imagine I'd be capable of such a thing…but we all do it, don't we? Contemplate murdering our parents.

EDWARD: No.

ADAM: LIAR! All children want to butcher the failures in their parents.

EDWARD: Not me.

ADAM: All you do is pretend…who for? For the people? All of them thinking of just as many terrible things as you or I, the only difference between someone like me and someone like…them, is that I acted on what they have all considered doing to those they despise. All of us know at least one person in the world who has considered our deaths with pleasure. Stood at the edge of the train tracks, do not tell me you have never considered sinister thoughts.

Silence.

79

ADAM: Why should anyone be considered a sinless man, when they themselves, think of the most heinous things imaginable. By now I think I've proven what one man is capable of.

EDWARD: We're done.

ADAM: …For now.

EDWARD exits.

END OF ISSUE II

MOVEMENT II ISSUE III

'Society'

ADAM studies the drawings on the table, the projection holds on an image of The Everyman Family, the mother, the father, the balloon, and the puppet. Some time passes, ADAM is left to his thoughts. EDWARD enters with two cups of water.

ADAM: ...Back so soon?

EDWARD: It's been a couple of days.

ADAM: Has it? I never had much use for time. I could never take hold with it, not without it blistering my hand.

Beat.

EDWARD: I brought you a drink.

ADAM: Thank you.

EDWARD sets the cups down.

Do you listen to the radio at all?

EDWARD: Now and then.

ADAM: I listen to it a lot, there isn't much else to do around here but listen, people think the talkers are the dangerous ones, but, no...it's those who listen, those are the ones we have to watch out for.

Beat.

EDWARD: And, which are you in your mind? Which are your followers?

ADAM: I have nothing to do with anything outside of these walls, you people have made sure of that. I've been both, but the listener seems to evoke the talker in me.

EDWARD: As did the chicken with the egg.

ADAM: Truth is a remarkable thing, isn't it? You'd think by now, in 2054, mankind would've learned from its history, just for a moment, just once. Yet here we sit, whispers of a global war, censorship of the 'false' And the masses? Not the least bit concerned. A conglomerate or a congress, their lines are as blurred as The Laos Front. No-one is concerned with the truth anymore, no-one cares.

EDWARD: What about you?

ADAM: What about me?

EDWARD: Well, when you killed all those people, did you give any concern for their truths?

ADAM: Killing those people wasn't about truth.

EDWARD: Then what was it about?

ADAM: …Well played.

Beat.

I killed my father first, as I'm sure you would have, the alcoholic who cared about nothing other than his vices. BORING!

82

ADAM: Next, one of my teachers at school, she desecrated my record with her own idiosyncratic nonsense and poor sense of taste. Next, three fellow students of mine, one who I didn't know by name, but knew of their endless ability to run their mouth. One who knew nothing other than how to fuck her way to the top of the class and another who, by definition, was a pig, and I despised his guts.

My mother was about her idleness, she once preached…with some intensity, the necessity of strength, she failed me. Lastly, the icon, the one who I aspired to work with, because I believed her words, the words of a star shining so beautifully in the darkness…it's funny how people will be indoctrinated by those around them, their friends, their countries, yet will cry foul when I should make the same effort. She died for her pride, as soon will everyone. My Modus Operandi is brutal and unending, Edward Cross. Four walls will not contain it, nor will your dwindling resolve.

EDWARD: You really are the talker, aren't you?

ADAM: That's because I listened as a boy, perhaps I'm compensating for that with you. Tell me, why do you think they keep sending you back in here?

ADAM leans in.

(Venomously) You are a sheep thrown to a wolf with a broken leg, we are effectively both hostages now, almost kin, dare I say.

EDWARD: I don't think so.

ADAM: Really? Then leave, and never return. I commend you in your defiance.

EDWARD: What if I don't want to?

Beat.

ADAM: …Now we're talking.

EDWARD: So, you killed those people, why? To prove a point?

ADAM: In a manner of speaking, and I think I have, don't you? Proved a point.

EDWARD: What point?

ADAM: If I had killed only my parents, my fellow students, and that pitiful excuse for a teacher…what do you think would've happened? Do you think there'd be an army of the greatest minds looking to unpack my fragile thoughts, had I not killed an international celebrity? No-one cared about the others, not till the seventh. Now, if we can extrapolate one thing from this ordeal, it's this…it will only be once the ultimate escalation occurs, that mankind will change. We do not change the world till we have been forced to change. It is simply our way.

A heart attack forces a middle-aged man to exercise, the destruction of two cities creates fear of mutually assured destruction across the world. As we consider the current political climate, lessons are only ever learned, after the fact. This coming one will be costly to us all, if I am correct.

EDWARD: You can't justify what you do because of nations that have been in a state of conflict for at least a hundred years.

ADAM: Anything can be justified against human history, I thought that was the noble thing to do.

EDWARD: Yes, when it doesn't serve your own ends.

ADAM: Academics want to be right as much as anybody else does. The economic devastation of the 2040's proved one thing, and one thing alone...when starved, man becomes a dog. The world has silently realised a grave truth, and it sits in the minds of children and elderly widows alike, now, how will it end, you ask? There are a number of theories, nuclear war, perhaps. Biological warfare, perhaps.

At the bottom of the list heralded by a conspiracist, was an option so sinister, it could not be seriously processed by anything other than an unhinged mind. The option was a weapon they called the MAD Bomb, something as devastating as a nuclear device, containing a psychedelic compound...turns the world inside out, biology and ecology...a fascinating concept don't you think?

The human story will end with the ego's cannibalism, madmen will expose themselves to be what they always were. Demons will be kings, and children will cry. That is the truth, unadulterated. Objective. Such a weapon would not exist, if the mind of one man was not lethal enough to kill himself. Imagine if such lethality could be weaponised.

EDWARD: By you?

ADAM: By anyone, that's the point. You see in this cup? The distortion in the water? Your own reflection looking back at you? It is at the bottom of this cup, the reflection, where the truth really is. No bias, no humanity, nothing besides what is there. Don't you think it'd be a simpler world? Living down there.

ADAM: I do enjoy a sense of irony...I imagine you, drowning with my face...isn't that strange? Would that be such a bad thing? Haven't you ever wanted that? To drown?

EDWARD: It's not the way I'd choose to go.

ADAM: No? Then how?

EDWARD: Well, I'd hope for something free of pain, I suppose.

ADAM: Humble, yet why is it deemed such an unreasonable request to expect such a thing from life?

EDWARD: Death is a moment; Life is a long time.

ADAM: Death is a moment, but what is dying then, if not the rest of your life?

EDWARD: And what do you envision doing with the rest of your life?

ADAM: When the end comes? Oh, I'm sure I'll think of something. Perhaps I'll be right for a change.

END OF ISSUE III

MOVEMENT II ISSUE IV

'See as I see'

EDWARD: …My father passed away.

ADAM: *(Leans forward)* Really?

EDWARD: Yeah.

ADAM: You're not fucking with me?

EDWARD: I wish I was.

Beat.

ADAM: No, you don't.

Silence.

EDWARD: How could you possibly believe that?

ADAM: Your silence. It's very telling, almost as telling as talking is, when a man hesitates, it's because you've discovered a truth. How did he die?

EDWARD: In hospital, in a coma. Not like yours.

ADAM: That's true, carbon monoxide does perform wonders. Did he suffer?

EDWARD: He was in a coma.

ADAM: Pity. Still, they say people in comas can still hear things, I bet you had some things to say, right? I can imagine you could be quite the talker too.

Beat.

ADAM: "How could you?", "I forgive you", "I hate you". Oh...so many things, did you pretend to forgive him? Just so he could finally succumb? Don't fret, we all lie to our loved ones.

EDWARD rolls his eyes.

You don't believe me? Is it such a wild thing?

EDWARD: Look...you want me to level with you, is that it? That's what you want...that's what *(indicating audience)* they want. Fine. I believe people can be shitty to one another, ok? I just don't see what that has to do with me being anything like you, I mean, I didn't kill anyone, so you managed to learn a bit about me, but you don't know fucking anything, you don't know a thing about me, you don't know a damn thing.

ADAM: ...The holocaust.

Beat.

EDWARD: ...Jesus fucking Christ. What does that have to do with anything?

ADAM: I was going to tell you. If you'll listen?

Beat.

EDWARD reaches in his pocket for a cigarette, he smokes.

EDWARD: Sure, go on ahead.

ADAM: You've already proven my point.

EDWARD: By lighting up a cigarette? We both smoke, is that where your analogy was heading? Did I just spoil that for you?

ADAM: You didn't smoke before, at least not so openly, meaning I must have had some part to play. However, you have proven my point, every single time you have come through that door. You have preconceived notions about how the world really works.

EDWARD: And you don't?

ADAM: No, I do. But at the very least, I'm aware of them.

EDWARD: Alright...tell me...what do I believe? What's the error of my ways?

EDWARD turns to the glass.

You're seeing this bullshit? I hope it's worth it, don't mind me, huh.

ADAM: When I mentioned a 'Holocaust' I was not specifically referring to the work of Adolf Hitler, no, the slave trade in North America, The extermination of the Native Americans, The Mongol Conquests, Stalin, Mussolini, the sterilisation of Tibetan culture in the Twentieth Century, I could go on... time and time again, leading back to the dawn of our species, a time in which we slaughtered our own counterparts, the story of man is an encyclopaedia of genocide by tribalism. We have deluded ourselves into believing political constitution, preserved by tradition, better warrants slaughter and illogical behaviour than so-called holy texts promising virgins or eternal paradise. Faith in God was the precursor to faith in System, both punishable by destruction.

89

ADAM: You should better heed my words. You have no idea what it's like to be torn apart, to lose your whole being, everything you are. They say that loss is relative, not to me. And very soon, not to anyone. Just wait.

END OF ISSUE IV

MOVEMENT II ISSUE V

'The Futility of The Pale Horse'

ADAM: You're beginning to understand, aren't you? I can't leave here, and you can't either. The difference between us, is, I have accepted the reality, you, still, have not. Which brings us to an additional game, chess is sufficient enough to prevent boredom, but hardly enough to interest me.

EDWARD: What game?

ADAM: You, in an attempt to get yourself out of this room, will do anything besides murdering me to get them to force you out. It's a game of chicken, but I must warn you, ambitions might be aligned, and not in your favour.

EDWARD: I can't imagine you had many friends growing up, eh?

ADAM: No, I didn't. Did you?

Beat.

EDWARD: No.

ADAM: Hmm, would you like to hear another theory?

EDWARD: …If you insist.

ADAM: Have you ever considered 'The Futility of The Pale Horse'?

EDWARD: What?

ADAM: "I looked, and there before me was a pale horse! Its rider was named Death, and Hades was following close behind him. They were given power over a fourth of the earth to kill by sword, famine and plague, and by the wild beasts of the earth." Revelation 6:8.

EDWARD: What about it? Why are we talking about this?

ADAM: Neither Gods nor Demons in their mythical might should require the riding of a horse...only a man would require such a thing, only a man kills by the sword.

EDWARD: How profound. I assume you've read the whole book?

ADAM: I found it quite hilarious, the vanity of man.

EDWARD: Vanity?

ADAM: Yes, your anger...it's so...vain. Look at you, ready to rip my head off and silence me, oh, how erotic the crime would be, how legendary...I'm almost tempted to let you.

Beat.

EDWARD: I would like to rip your fucking head off.

ADAM laughs hysterically, EDWARD joins in, the pair laugh as one.

ADAM: You're trying to hurt me?

EDWARD: I'm trying.

ADAM: That was a good one.

EDWARD: Thank you.

ADAM: It seems we both have a habit.

EDWARD: So it seems.

ADAM: You know what I'm going to say, don't you?

EDWARD: Don't say it. I'm warning you. I wouldn't.

ADAM: Oh no.

EDWARD: You think I'm joking; *(Calmly)* I'll fucking kill you...right here. I'll fucking do it.

ADAM: With what? Your hands? I don't think so.

EDWARD: No?

ADAM: No.

EDWARD: Ok, how about this...

EDWARD reveals a small handgun.

I could shoot some holes in you, that could be fun.

ADAM: It could be fun, because I'm going to say it.

Beat.

In fact, that's the best part...I don't even have to.

EDWARD lunges forward towards ADAM, throwing him against the table.

END OF ISSUE V

MOVEMENT II ISSUE VI

'Indoctrination'

EDWARD: Keep talking you piece of shit…go on.

ADAM: Ooh…I am frightened…or perhaps…flattered. Did you bring that all the way in here, just for me?

EDWARD: Get the fuck out of my head.

ADAM: I'm not in there, it's just you, it's always been just you…the truth is terrifying, so, the human in you…it wants to kill the truth, but look…ssh…look! Where are they? Where are our masters? Nowhere to be seen, it's just you and me…but to them…it's just me.

EDWARD backs away.

…Welcome to my world.

"Welcome to my world" as performed by Jim Reeves plays as ADAM begins to dance towards EDWARD, the latter of which is confused, disorientated, lost.

EDWARD: Where's that coming from!?

ADAM: YOU CAN HEAR IT!? AHHHHHHHHHHH WOOOOOOHOOOOOO YOU CAN FUCKING HEAR THE FUCKING MUSIC! OH GOD! I'M NOT THE FUCKING ONLY ONE! HA HA HA! I'M NOT CRAZY! I KNEW IT! I KNEW IT WAS REAL! YES!

ADAM celebrates, meanwhile, EDWARD attempts to escape, the room is locked.

EDWARD: LET ME OUT! LET ME THE FUCK OUT OF HERE! WHAT THE HELL IS THIS! SOMEONE PLEASE!

The lights fade to black, the music carries us forward, before the sound of an early air raid warning fills the air.

END OF ISSUE VI

MOVEMENT II ISSUE VII

'Juggernaut'

In darkness. ADAM rises, convulsing, clutching his head. His brain is twisted by the effects of a sinister weapon. A red dusky light emerges in the room, he stares up at the red light before him, like a rabid animal.

ADAM: …The light glows black and the darkness shines brightly. Hold on, Ahab did, to the white whale so tightly. Oh, it's so beautiful. Red and hot and vengeful, terrifying, the bleeding wave over the world. Children in the streets, holding their hands up to chaos. To never know tyranny is a life of peace, then their deaths are as worthy as anyone's. How right, the children shall be spared my vengeance in this new world.

Every man will be accountable to himself now. Only to himself, bees will walk the earth, elephants will know the clouds…men will know ambition, and opportunity. It is truly magnificent. Chaos is without prejudice, but, for too long, without one who could play her strings. Till I…till you. Why replace one legend with another? The redemption of a fallen man bestowed his saviour with his father's name. Ingenious.

I am then, Edward. Oh, the succulence, the taste of the sound! Free of shame. Yet not of promises. I will wear your name too. And you, shall be legend, myth, despised and adored, yet never absolved. You shall dance on the ashes of your blindness for an eternity. You will carve the eyes of the blind out at my will, you will be the hands to my mind, the will to my spirit. We shall reshape the world together, gloriously. For what is the name of Adam Apocalypse? But words in a story. Who told you the story was true? Who formed the narrative of nonsense?

97

ADAM: What those of which are believed, will be believed always. And now, I know my purpose. One shall at last share the nightmare's fever with me.

The dusky light dies as the radio returns with a heavy crackle, one last time.

COLIN: The sins of the father.

BRIAN: Are the sins, of the world.

END OF ISSUE VII

NOTES ON MOVEMENT III CHAPTER I

Intended Performance Style: Expressionistic. Physical. Performative. Loud. Animated. Emotive.

Intended Mise-En-Scene: Decadent. Surrealistic. Psychological. Dystopian. Alive. Colourful. Insane. Wonderous.

During this opening chapter of the third movement, we are introduced to what appears to be a post-apocalyptic take upon the region of Hereford, England. A stranger 'Edward Cross' arrives in the territory of 'New Albion' Who seeks an audience with a powerful king 'The Death Merchant' To offer his supposed abilities as a bounty hunter, to kill an infamous charismatic terrorist, 'Adam Apocalypse'

Although there are many in the populace of New Albion who remember the events that led to the third and final World War. Those simply too young to remember, have all but forgotten the world that existed before. At least at a conscious level. The characters, regardless of the audiences' perception of this reality, are all suffering with severe psychedelic effects. Though the characters themselves are ultimately unaware of this.

Some have been affected more than others, any pre-existing mental health conditions have been dangerously exacerbated. In the region of Hereford, the impact of the MAD bombs has perverted the rise of a new civilisation, fragmented, disorganised, and even at times, nonsensical. Picture a flower, having grown in bad soil, stunted, and doomed, that is the world of this movement.

Following on from Movement II, Adam has tortured his former 'captor' Edward, into becoming a defacto symbol of a dangerous cult. Meanwhile, he has taken Edward's name, journeyed across this dystopian world, and has become an anti-hero through his wanderings. Creating a character and using his influence to build a reputation worthy of an audience with 'The Death Merchant'

A man once famed for his ability to destroy threats from the undesirable kind, building a nation with a small amassed army. Ultimately, in a genius political manuver, Edward is able to use 'Adam Apocalypse' to provoke the people of New Albion into an uprising, utilising every opportunity afforded to him by the foolishness and faith of those surrounding him, Edward *(The true Adam)* contradicts the intricacies of his philosophies to seize true power for himself, furthering his role as our unreliable narrator.

There are clear indicators throughout the text that suggest this fantasy is once again a dystopian dream to Adam Everyman. The implausibility of his plot to take the throne, the lack of challenge in his efforts, in addition to various subtle contradictions and references throughout all movements of the work which suggest a fictitious foundation for the reality of the future. There is a definitive answer as to the question "Is Movement III set in the real world? Or within Adam's mind?" However, on the part of the author, the answer will never be revealed in these pages.

CHARACTERS

ADAM APOCALYPSE: The puppet, the prince of madness, the mask of the master. *(If applicable, played by the same actor as EDWARD in Movement II.)*

EDWARD: Legacy of the father, in a world of his own. *(If applicable, played by the same actor as ADAM in Movement II.)*

ELLIOT: Late Teens, The sins of the father, the reasonable child. *(If applicable, played by the same actor as ELLEN in Movement I.)*

THE DEATH MERCHANT: A middle-aged king, overweight and blind to empathy. *(If applicable, played by the same actor as BOSS in movement I.)*

GODFEAR: Fame is often found in the foolish. An apostle of a fragmented religion. *(If applicable, played by the same actor as FATHER in Movement I.)*

WORLD PAINTERS: A tight knit ensemble of individuals who colour the world written in black and white. Fulfilling all other roles that are not individually assigned to another.

COLIN: An intellectual, a man who accepts and settles with the 'facts'.

BRIAN: A radical man of conjecture and chaos.

NEW ALBION GLOSSARY

(Applies to both Chapter 1 and Chapter 2)

New Albion: The region of Hereford, as first named in the manifesto of 'The Liberal Repatriation Group', 2043. Occupied by The Death Merchant's own army of bounty hunters and mercenaries in 2056, they have since founded a nation, becoming ministers, ceremonial guards and state police.

The New Ancient Apostles: The reformed and reunified Christian church. An organisation, although in its infancy, that utterly rejects the failings of man's involvement in the organisation of religious intuitions and seeks to offer a pure, self-sacrificing organisation of missionaries, who bring the word of God to the numerous isolated settlements outside of The Capital of New Albion, Manning Station.

The Final Testament: In the wake of the Armageddon of 2054, those who hid in the shadows, saved only by their belief in a Christian God wrote a series of religious declarations which became known as 'The Final Testament' thanks to the reunification of the Christian faith in 2060.

Gretchling: A stunted humanoid creature, derived from researcher Dr. Gretchen Walters, who in 2057, met a savage end by her own discovery.

The Madlands: Formerly known as the region of The Brecon Beacons', Wales. The Madlands is the western most territory of New Albion. Shrouded in a thick green haze, the ground saturated like marshland. This unholy place is feared by many of the locals for being home to The Cult of Adam. Originally named by celebrity podcast presenters Colin Peterson and Brian Barnes, this region is the most dangerous territory in New Albion, home to many mysteries.

The Northern Wastes: Formerly known as the region of Greater Manchester.

Penny Fetcher: A person of low wealth or social status, lacking an understanding of etiquette.

The Southern Shit Knife: A coastal region of England stretching from Penzance to Portsmouth.

The Undesirable Kind: A New Albionic' term for marauder, bandit, cutthroat or highwaymen.

THE SYMPHONY OF ADAM APOCALYPSE

MOVEMENT THREE

CHAPTER I

'Responsibility'

MOVEMENT III ISSUE I

'A Damned Dystopia'

2064, following the collapse of civilisation after a third and final world war. The skies above the former United Kingdom are a forever swirling red and black hurricane, dust storms are common, yet gentle dances of rain are permitted, so water, although remaining a contested issue in the barren wasteland, is more plentiful than one might expect. The Cascadian Abyss, formerly known as the area of Hereford. GODFEAR enters, the sound of dust on the greenhouse wind. Light attire, a mark of 'The New Ancient Apostles' a holy order, built out of the remnants of three Christian based faiths. He removes his hood, looking to the destruction of the wastes before him, an old church still stands. GODFEAR kneels, glancing up. For a brief moment, a pure light welcomes him. From a brown satchel, he removes 'The Final Testament' a bible esque book, holding it tightly in his grip.

GODFEAR: How shameful a waste, all the years of mankind.

EDWARD enters, dressed in ragged long attire, fit for purpose. Tattered skull and bones makeup upon his face, both men keep at their distance.

You will find no treasures here, marauder. At least none of gold or glory.

EDWARD: I do enjoy glory. But, I am no marauder, merely a wanderer, a teller of tales. Much like yourself. It's been a while since I've seen one of you boys around.

GODFEAR: There are few of us left outside the capital these days.

EDWARD: So it seems. I always enjoy the little names you assign yourselves, tell me, what's yours?

GODFEAR: Godfear.

Edward smiles.

Amusing, is it?

EDWARD: Irony is all we have these days, you can ignore it, shun it, or package it into something you can use.

Beat.

GODFEAR: Where are you from?

EDWARD: Nowhere, but also not from here.

GODFEAR: Then allow me to give you a piece of advice, 'man from nowhere'. There are far stranger names in these times than mine, belonging to far less tolerant men, that I can assure you.

EDWARD: Ah, well, I did hear one name which might satisfy your criteria...perhaps you're familiar with it?

GODFEAR: And what name would that be?

EDWARD: 'Adam Apocalypse' ?

Silence.

GODFEAR: We do not speak that name so openly. It is considered an ill omen.

EDWARD: You must forgive me.

GODFEAR: No, you must forgive yourself. It won't be my life that'll be forfeit, although I would ordinarily offer to give it freely in place of yours out of duty... I'm afraid it is no longer mine to give.

EDWARD: Trouble?

GODFEAR: Well, none that I could offer. I am to walk a path of atonement through 'The Madlands', and face the ill omen himself. Somehow, I am expected to convince him to change from his path. To see the light.

EDWARD: Sounds like someone wants you dead.

GODFEAR: It is the nature of the atonement.

EDWARD: Surely out here, everyone is atoning for something.

GODFEAR: Guilt and atonement are not the same thing. I consider going to my death a great honour.

EDWARD: And tell me, what did you do to earn this "Great honour."?

GODFEAR: I allowed myself to feel anger.

Beat.

EDWARD: I hate to spoil your day with philosophical debate, here of all places, but surely everyone who has ever lived has felt such a thing? Catch your foot on the wrong piece of debris strewn around here, well, a man could earn a thousand of these atonements for that alone.

GODFEAR: It was that manner of thinking that condemned green trees to our imagination for all eternity. The internal must no longer be forgiven in the eyes of God.

EDWARD doesn't appear convinced.

You must think I'm mad, yes?

EDWARD: Oh no, my friend. I know exactly what you mean…more than you could imagine.

GODFEAR: What about you? I doubt you came from wherever you did to admire this old building…stood for centuries, endured man's wars, and woes…and even now, when everything else falls to the fire, enough of it still stands. "Hope."

EDWARD: Or warning?

Beat.

EDWARD: I'm on my way to the capital, to see 'The Death Merchant'. Or whichever of the thirty names precedes an audience with the man.

GODFEAR: 'Master and Lord', there are many names for 'The Death Merchant' An audience with him personally? I won't ask questions where they're not wanted, but-

EDWARD: Bounty Hunter.

GODFEAR: Ah, well forgive me when I say I wouldn't have believed it unless I'd heard it from you.

EDWARD: Why not?

GODFEAR: Well, I'm no expert, but, your frame is all wrong, far too light, doesn't look like you've tumbled with too many undesirables from where I'm standing. You must be quite the talker.

EDWARD: ...Spent much time around that sort, have you?

GODFEAR: More than you would think, in another life, yes.

EDWARD: Well, the pen is mightier than the sword once spoken.

GODFEAR: Edward Bulwer-Lytton. Well, almost. An educated man too, eh? Still, it's not my place to question a man's story. Your business is your own.

EDWARD: Perhaps appearances can be deceiving? Both Church and Man are as guilty as they come in that regard, wouldn't you agree?

GODFEAR: Perhaps. So, who are you hunting?

EDWARD: The same prey as you, apparently.

GODFEAR: You must have a death wish, at least that would explain the makeup.

EDWARD: The makeup is a personal choice... *(He approaches)*. When you are standing face to face with death itself, it is only his reflection that might terrify his soul.

Beat.

Well, this has been, enlightening...as a token of respect, and for your sake, I hope that I find him first.

GODFEAR: And as a token of duty, I hope you don't. Safe travels to you...?

EDWARD: Edward Cross.

GODFEAR: Travel by light, and stay vigilant on the road. New Albion is a strange place.

END OF ISSUE I

MOVEMENT III ISSUE II

'New Albion'

A short classical score adjoined with a simple sketch. A WORLD PAINTER enters, leaving trash across the space. Behind them, a second PAINTER enters, who tires of constantly cleaning their waste into a bin at the climax of the piece, they pour the bin out onto the floor. The world is doomed. COLIN and BRIAN emerge on the radio. As the radio presenters do battle, our WORLD PAINTERS exit.

COLIN: With the rate of attacks across The Cascadian Abyss once again on the rise, further pressure is being placed on Issac Hornell, otherwise known as 'The Death Merchant', to allocate further resources into the manhunt for dystopian state undesirable, 'Adam Apocalypse'. Brian, any thoughts? DON'T TOUCH MY FUCKING HAM!

BRIAN: It's a simple one, Colin. President Death and his government of little butterflies is once again up to some black ops shit across the abyss. I'm talking about bases on the moon levels of shit here, I'm talking Bigfoot's relationship with Jesus. My sources tell me things, I'm sorry they're not up to par with your Godly Gestapo types at The New Ancient Apostles, GOD HELP THEM! I heard yet another bounty hunter has made his way into the territory. More on this to follow, don't look at me like that Colin, my sources are reliable, my people are glued in, you know?

COLIN: Glued?

BRIAN: Clued.

COLIN: You said, "Glued."

BRIAN: No, I didn't. You must be hearing things. ARE YOU FUCKING CRAZY!? ARE YOU FUCKING INSANE OR SOMETHING!? ARE YOU HEARING THINGS, COLIN!?

COLIN: Yeah, I did, things like "Glued." TOUCH MY FUCKING HAM ONE MORE TIME AND I WILL SLICE OUT YOUR INNARDS!

Beat.

BRIAN: There's always whispers they try and put into our words, people.

COLIN: Today's radio broadcast has been brought to you by Madison Hackett's beef pies...79% beef, the rest is up to you...and the trash compactor's rejects on Friday.

BRIAN: Oh also, we need someone with engineering skills in the region of Manning Station, THE SHINING CAPITAL! If those prick guards of Death didn't smash up my projector, I'd roll that shit right onto his little palace all over again! Believe the truth people! The Cult of Adam is just like Operation Northwoods all over again, they know an attack is coming, they let it manifest itself, then boom, two words RE-ELECTION. You heard it here first. And that's just the thing, HEAR ME PEOPLE, AND DESPAIR...also, the pies are pretty good. Why are you looking at me like-?

The radio dies.

The Coastal Town of Manning Station. The seat of power in The Cascadian Abyss and New Albion. THE DEATH MERCHANT enters, escorted by ELLIOT. The Merchant's eyes are bandaged and bloody, a strange sweaty nature about him. Upon his head, a rust ridden metallic crown, a badge of his office. ELLIOT, dressed for action as a guide and scavenger, a member of her father's force.

DEATH: Where is this doctor of yours?

ELLIOT: He'll be here in a matter of days, I'm sure he's just delayed.

DEATH: Fearmongering. It does little more than to make the roads less traversable than wet mud against a rising tide. I should have them put to death.

ELLIOT: Who?

DEATH: Those who spread fear and anarchy through our lands. And those...horses speaking as men on the radio.

ELLIOT: Oh yes, put them all to death. I'm sure that'll do well to have you re-elected. Perhaps you would be wise to choose your words more carefully in a public forum.

DEATH: Imagine if I no longer required re-election, I would have so much more time for the people. They'd love me. Their minds would be so unburdened.

ELLIOT: If you no longer require re-election. You do not have the people. Besides, it seems this commotion has worked in your favour. You need not pretend otherwise, father of mine.

DEATH: Favour often turns to frustration. It's bad enough they expect me to chase ghosts of the past. Have they no pity for what they think we have endured? Where is their sense of compassion?

ELLIOT: Lies do not often allow for pity.

Beat.

A WORLD PAINTER enters as a guard.

PAINTER: There is a man at the gates asking to meet with 'The Great Merchant of Death'. He proclaims to be 'The Pacifist' a name of legend in the South, and he also claims he has an interest in the matter of 'Adam Apocalypse'.

Beat.

111

DEATH: *(To Elliot)* Claims at the feet of The Death Merchant...They still speak of me as if I still had leverage over that game of commodities. If they knew better, they'd know a man cannot see everything without his eyes. Do they think I've forgotten my responsibilities to them?

ELLIOT: In order to forget, you must have first known something to begin with, Father. Besides, you stopped using them long before. Least now, you can tell them yourself. *(To Painter)* Bring him in.

The PAINTER exits.

DEATH: Does something trouble you, my daughter?

ELLIOT: No.

DEATH: Take my hand.

DEATH reaches out with his hand; ELLIOT reluctantly places her hands in his.

I promise you; I will do all in my power to find him. Not for the people, but for you. And when the time comes...you will tell them, won't you? That I tried?

Beat.

ELLIOT snatches her hand back.

ELLIOT: Spare me your performance, I will play the game for them, but do not think for one second that I myself will be played.

ELLIOT exits.

DEATH: They say he never kills. The Pacifist. Showed up out of nowhere around six years ago, a settlement on the southern shit knife. The way the story goes, this town in the desolate wastes was being harassed by 'The Undesirable Kind' A term of endearment for the lost and the reviled. These men were taking what they couldn't fuck, and fucking what they couldn't carry. This Pacifist never raised a weapon to them, but broke their legs and took their cocks.

So, a legend was born. You know the world has truly fallen when that's what qualifies you to be a pacifist around here. But that's how it goes in New Albion, yeah, you heard me. In a time long passed, a socialist party hellbent on saving the edge of the end, tried to reform the sweltering mess of the United Kingdom. Little did they realise, a Utopia and a Dystopia can both be the same thing. So, when the whole world burst into flames, those fools had no fires of their own at which they could sit and sing and celebrate in their rhetoric.

Not without a score of third degree burns and a score of cysts across your body like a boiling strew of Gretchling tumours. Now mutants and monsters and men live and die as they always have, and I have done my utmost to rebuild the world, at great personal cost. I've never seen anything like that vile creature who bears the name of 'Adam' Just about everyone who's left knows about him, has been burned by him.

They say the lonely and abandoned revere him as a God, they say he whispers to them on gales that blow from the West. I never used to believe such stories. Not till he came for my daughter.

The DEATH MERCHANT reaches out in anguish.

Took her right from me…

…I never saw her again. If I'd known she was…I would have done something, if she was mad, I WOULD HAVE KNOWN!

DEATH: I spent so many years, so long, wandering, commanding the deaths of the many to afford the hunt of one animal. Thankfully, my people supported me with their strength. When at last I faced him, he took my sight from me, broke my body, but left my mind intact and nursed me just well enough so that I might survive. In darkness I called for him, and his voice...was so gentle. I begged him to tell me where my daughter was...then I heard her speak...and then they were gone, forever.

At last, I could walk into the night no more. Instead, here I sit, on a throne of silence, nothing more than a useless fool! With only the company of penny fetchers and undesirables to hunt down this dog! I want him found, I want to reach out with my hands and squeeze the life from him as if I was squeezing fluid from the head of a spot.

The DEATH MERCHANT squeezes his head...broken.

Have I satisfied your curiosity? Or would you humour my proposal in a great game of death?

EDWARD comes into the light, having been concealed in darkness till this point.

EDWARD: I see you like to dance with your words. Like a politician. You go by many names, King, President, Merchant... I, however, do not dance. Not for a king, for a man of God, for no-one. Mutually assured profit has brought us together, and I will make you an offer. But, my glorious and esteemed friend, should you not take advantage of my offering, should you choose greed over the good of your people, be cautious, my friend, for they will eat you, if you do not distract them from their humanity.

DEATH: That's a lot of dancing for one who claims not to dance.

EDWARD: I am but a man.

DEATH: Aren't we all? But, let us talk as sensible men at the very least, what is it you want? Name it, what prize is worth the price of death?

EDWARD: I understand you have a ship?

DEATH: I do.

EDWARD: Does it work?

DEATH: It floats, more than can be said for most of my fleet these days. You can thank 'Adam' and his band of merry men for that.

EDWARD: Your ship will be my payment. The one still afloat, that is.

Beat.

DEATH: That is no small price to pay.

EDWARD: But the continued slaughter of your own electorate is?

Beat.

DEATH: Strange, your voice is somehow as both harsh and soft as his was. What use is a boat to a bounty hunter of all trades?

EDWARD: That's not your concern, if that should change, consider it an ill omen for you.

DEATH: When kings carry ill omens, mutually assured destruction is often inevitable.

EDWARD: You are no king.

Beat.

Men do not elect kings to power, not out of admiration or pity.

115

EDWARD: Yeah, well, if that's true, then why are you still alive? Or what about the people out there?

ADAM: Notice I choose my words carefully, destruction, not death. To truly silence your enemies, you must have taken their tongue, forcibly. That was the way of the ancient world, and I am sure that very soon, so shall it be again. However, in this moment that we find ourselves in, why should I kill you? When I can destroy you with the blessing of law and a false moral compass dictated by a failing society. I can silence you without uttering a word, destroy your entire life if I so choose, for a mistake you may have made a lifetime ago, it's a perfect killing machine...the technological society of the last days of mankind.

EDWARD: That doesn't help me understand.

ADAM: Oh no, it does, you aren't listening.

EDWARD: Listening? All you do is talk, that's all you do! That's all you're fucking capable of!

Beat.

ADAM: Seems we both have a temper. I don't hate you, Edward. Because you don't understand, you've never had any reason to. A perfect life, a beautiful daughter...

EDWARD: How did you know about that-

ADAM: She is beautiful. Brown hair, big brown eyes...truly. My favourite.

EDWARD: We're done here...

EDWARD stands.

DEATH: Perhaps. Answer me this; Why you? I have lost countless men chasing this demon across the abyss. Your voice does not tell me tales of bravery, but instead, it tells me yours is a tale of sadness.

EDWARD: We all have our demons and deceptions. A bounty hunter is no exception.

DEATH: You are no bounty hunter.

Beat.

You do not kill for money. 'Pacifist'.

EDWARD: No, but the world keeps on turning and I stake my claim anyway.

Beat.

DEATH: A moral claim?

EDWARD: A claim in its own right.

DEATH: A fool's claim!

EDWARD: A claim then, still. In its own right.

DEATH: Well then, you are no bounty hunter and I am no king. Very well, I accept. But…stories are important things, a story told well, becomes the truth, even if it is a lie. A story such as yours, for example. If you are to cross 'The Madlands' into his domain. You will need a guide. And I will need insurance.

EDWARD: A dog or a Gretchling will suffice, your insurance can be your right to escape should the masses turn on you.

DEATH: No-one empathises with a dead Gretchling. Daughter!?

ELLIOT enters.

116

ELLIOT: Father?

DEATH: This is Elliot Hornell, my eldest. Elliot, 'The Pacifist' Edward Cross.

Beat.

My daughter will be the one to take you through 'The Madlands.'

ELLIOT: I will not.

DEATH: You will do as I command.

ELLIOT: I am not yours to-

DEATH: You will do as I say! Or I will find me a daughter who will! For far too long you have made judgements of me your pastime against my rule. Since you think you can do a better job, here is your chance to win the hearts and minds of the people you so long to love. Forgive me, Pacifist. She has already dishonoured me in public, I see no reason not to silence her there also.

Beat.

ELLIOT: And if I should not return?

DEATH: The realm will grieve in my favour. That, Pacifist, will be my insurance.

ELLIOT approaches DEATH, she speaks softly.

ELLIOT: And your favour shall perish as a despicable frustration. Father of mine.

ELLIOT exits, she bows.

DEATH: Remember, Pacifist. Alive

117

EDWARD: Your daughter? I will try.

EDWARD exits. DEATH clenches his fist in anger.

END OF ISSUE II

MOVEMENT III ISSUE III

'Reflections of The Anarchist'

A short distance to the North of Manning Station's borders. The radio returns.

COLIN: It begs the question, doesn't it? Just where this 'Adam Apocalypse' originated from, I heard he was once a musician who lost faith in pre-calamity society.

BRIAN: I heard he was a humanoid robot from the year 2099, sent back in time to usher in the great calamity by the lizard people of the world of tomorrow.

Beat.

The lesson is; Don't believe everything you hear people. You heard it here first. ARE YOU LISTENING!?

COLIN: ...Anyway, this radio broadcast is brought to you by 'Caucasian Fragrance' because the rest of you out there, are worth the privilege.

BRIAN: Don't you think these sponsors are a little-ORDINARY!?

COLIN: I think the real question on our minds is, who is this 'Adam Apocalypse'. What is his plan? Is he simply a madman hellbent on the destruction of all things? Or...

BRIAN: One of the lizard people.

Beat.

COLIN: Play the fucking music, Brian. You're reading out the sponsors from now on.

BRIAN: I've got just the thing.

To the tune of 'Happy Together' by The Turtles. ADAM APOCALYPSE enters, a thick pair of aviators upon his face. He carries with him a large steel golf club, dancing to the music whilst drinking from a red American party cup. He plays a few rounds of golf, before raising his cup, Two WORLD PAINTERS rush in, bowing before the lord of madness, they refill his beverage. A third PAINTER enters, carrying a note.

PAINTER: I saw him! With my own eyes! I saw him! The Bounty Hunter and his bones, sharing the road with a young woman.

EDWARD: A woman? Death's own daughter, no less?

PAINTER: As your prophecy has predicted. What will we do now, O' brilliant one?

ADAM: The world is shit! Shit with sick, sick with shit. So it has been since the dawn of our time. In my youth, I dreamed of a world, so divine, majestic, and beautiful…it could have only ever been a dream. At least, in their minds. For the dream was poisoned with tales of alcoholics, dead mothers and tales told in sound and music…my life was an experience of the many movements of destruction, the woeful symphony of mankind. *(Clutching his head)* My mother, my beautiful, paragon angel… I'd often come home; my mother would barricade us inside my room for hours. Those doors would shake and rattle and scream as the alcoholic searched the house for us.

I was so scared. I asked her, my mother, why she was crying. She smiled at me and said 'Imagine you could be anybody in the world, anyone who has ever lived, who would you be? So, I made my choice, I chose to be the man who could've saved her, and failing that…the man who would stop at nothing to avenge her. So, I ask of you, my ever faithful, will you help me avenge her? Will you let me help you avenge yourselves? Will you stand with me now and choke the life from the cancer of man that they would see become once again, a world so malignant and magnificent in their view?

120

ADAM: For all those you've loved and lost. They choose to honour Death with a crown, still speaking as if this is their world…their insolence is matched only by their dedication to build a monstrous monument to the damned. I would ask you, my friends, travel these lands, burn every brick, pluck every feather, dissolve every hope. If they will not see the future, we shall remind them of the fires of their past.

GODFEAR enters.

GODFEAR: Words of one who still might know the light…

The WORLD PAINTERS cover ADAM, hissing at this intruder. They all inch forward, slowly moving towards GODFEAR.

ADAM: No!

GODFEAR: …Even, if he is truly one of darkness.

The WORLD PAINTERS back away.

ADAM: Do you speak for your God, sir?

GODFEAR: I do, sir.

ADAM: Yes, sir. Good, sir. I am glad, sir. Yes, sir. No, sir. Tell me…sir…am I evil because I have slaughtered?

GODFEAR: Yes.

ADAM: And has your lord, your God, not slaughtered? Did he not set the sky on fire and damn both the good and bad in a somewhat unforgiving and anticlimactic rapture?

GODFEAR: Yes.

ADAM: Then, tell me sir, if you would be so good, sir, if you would be so kind, sir…an answer…am I evil because I am blasphemous?

121

GODFEAR: Yes.

ADAM: And has your lord, your God, not been blasphemous? Surely a Lord that is all truthful would only have need for but one testament? No, instead he works as I do, through the broken and helpless. With the prerequisites for your saviour being so pathetic for even the most lesser of beings to aspire to, I would even be a better choice of candidate for your God.

GODFEAR: Even if it should mean my death. You, sir, are not my God.

ADAM: And your God is **not**. But tell me, in this moment, I could order you struck down into the black. I could have you burned till you beg me as your God for the release of death. I could cut you, chop you, twist you, turn you...can your God do any of these things? *(Godfear is silent)*. No answer? Surely, he did not send you to me so...underprepared. I'm insulted. Then again, he wasn't there for me either, even though I asked for him, he never came.

ADAM approaches GODFEAR, stroking his face.

Why not tell me the truth, Godfearing man? You came to me for salvation. A gentle butterfly placing the trust of his life in the hands of a stranger...the preacher does take many forms, but, unfortunately for you...

ADAM grabs GODFEAR's face tightly.

God killed me, condemned me to servitude and destruction. And for that I shall kill and condemn you. Take him!

A PAINTER grabs GODFEAR.

PAINTER: Shall we throw him into the abyss?

ADAM: No. I will take him back with me.

PAINTER: And what of the bounty hunter?

122

ADAM: Let him see the world is burning. Bring fire to the hills, fire to their hearts...fire, to their God.

ALL exit.

END OF ISSUE III

MOVEMENT III ISSUE IV

'The World is Burning'

A plateau. Where a venture begins. EDWARD enters, a black balaclava to protect his face against dust. A thick rucksack with a thick brown journal on show with a ragged pencil attached to it by a piece of string. Beside him, ELLIOT, dressed for the road, a pair of steampunk esque goggles attached to her forehead. She has a small snub-nosed pistol.

ELLIOT: You really don't do subtle, do you?

EDWARD: Neither does your father.

ELLIOT: Yeah, I noticed. What's with the makeup? I've been meaning to ask.

EDWARD: Let's just say I have an ironic sense of humour.

ELLIOT: It's some sense of humour alright…where did you get it from?

EDWARD: My father, that was…before.

ELLIOT: Before the war? I can hardly remember it. Flying cars, convenient food and giant machines that could take you to the stars. It must have been something to watch burn.

EDWARD: Oh, you wouldn't believe it.

ELLIOT looks out to the desolate wastes, to her eyes, it is the only home she has ever known.

ELLIOT: Tell me…

As EDWARD tells her, ELLIOT dreams of this distant world, till the story turns without hope, and her dream dies with it.

EDWARD: It was seemingly a paradise, green fields, blue skies...trees rustling in an unburning wind. The colour was overwhelming, sunflowers as tall as a man, the sound of a freighter on its way to Mars, the distant rumble of the engines singing over a purple dawn. In the cities, the greatest minds who had ever lived. At a mere gesture or command, clean, rich, cool water...more food than the sum of a thousand hunts. In one sitting.

ELLIOT: It must have been paradise.

EDWARD: It must have looked that way, from an outside eye. Yet for all their magnificence, the sum of their feast was greed. They destroyed the world for millions before they did it to themselves. When the sky set ablaze and the wealthy were driven into starvation and poverty, it was only the true survivors of the old who could become leaders of the new. And even with everything lost...still the maddened minds of maddened men desired their fatal flaws rebuilt.

Beat.

You dream of the old, because you have never known it. Others dream of the old, because they have. You know what your father is, I envy your ignorance...to truly believe he is anything but the result of a cycle that has been played out for thousands of years. You're right to fear for him, even despite that you know what he truly is. It's admirable, that although it has all you've ever known, barbarity against the innocent is not some simple fact of life in your eyes.

ELLIOT: What are you trying to say?

EDWARD: Whatever happens out here, it changes nothing for your father. Mark my words.

ELLIOT exits. EDWARD smiles as he wanders behind her, trailing through the wastes. Our radio presenters return.

COLIN: The world is burning! In a gruesome string of terror attacks upon settlements from across the Cascadian abyss, all visible from the walls of the capital, has left the realm in uproar! The Cult of Adam has claimed official responsibility for the attacks, in a statement issued by the Junior Adjutant of The Albion Guard, Anton Yellowfever stated "There is no cause for alarm, but alarm may be apparent anyway." President-King Hornell is working every moment to devise a strategy to counter this barbarity, New Albion will persevere, we, will persevere. Brian?

BRIAN: I've got two words for you, Colin "Population Control."

COLIN: Don't be ridiculous. Now, folks, I'm sure everything will be under control in a matter of hours, we all just need to remain calm.

BRIAN: REMAIN CALM!

COLIN: ... Why?

BRIAN: I just wanted to show people what not to do.

COLIN: This broadcast is brought to you by 'Genghis Khan's nightlights for children' because if your kid is going to be traumatised, it might as well involve an awesome explosion.

ELLIOT and EDWARD return. The WORLD PAINTERS form a well.

ELLIOT: There is a superstition about The Madlands. They say for one to pass through them, you must consume the water. They say the water opens your mind, so that he might indoctrinate you as you travel through the green haze. To not drink it is to submit yourself to the terrors within. The power of the mind can summon the most terrifying fantasies, wouldn't you agree?

126

EDWARD: The mind cannot conjure the impossible, if terror lays within the heart, then it also lays before the eye. Faith is a cry from fear, nothing more.

ELLIOT: And you know no fear?

Beat.

EDWARD: I don't allow it to lead me to places where I don't belong.

ELLIOT: I'm here because my father has no-one else to send.

EDWARD: Perhaps you'd have been wise to refuse him?

Beat.

ELLIOT: I've seen what my father does to those he deems 'wiser' than himself.

EDWARD: Well then, drink on up. Don't let me stop you.

ELLIOT: You have quite the mouth on you, do you know that?

EDWARD: It comes with experience.

ELLIOT: Experience of being an asshole?

EDWARD: If you knew better where I've come from, what I've seen, you would think twice about speaking to me like that.

Beat.

ELLIOT: Try me.

EDWARD: You think because you've lived the horrors of an ordinary life in this world, that you know all there is to know, and it gives you the right to be arrogant. When the truth is, you know nothing of this world, nothing of horror.

EDWARD: A couple of years ago I was journeying through the capital, I'm one of a select few who's been made it through there alive, folks from all around outside the city have stories about what it's like once you get past the rubble and ash fields. Some say there's a utopian society formed from the remnants of the surviving government. Others, that it's a land overrun with the undead. All the stories, every single one you ever heard. They're all wrong. There's nothing in there, it's just a haze of red firestorms, blazing sour green bile from the earth beneath...

...There was one thing, something that scared me still into tears. A street that had a still standing wall sprayed in black graffiti 'The Street of Tiny Hands', I was trying to make my way through that hell storm as fast as I could, I turned the corner, and that whole road leading West was filled to the brim with what appeared to be children's bodies. They were piled upon one another like sandbags. Occasionally, like growing daisies, there'd be an upright hand, bloodied and blackened by fire. Sometimes, I'd swear the hands were moving.

There was no way around for miles, the only way was to walk over them, and their bones were somehow so soft that their bodies would break beneath your feet. I walked for miles, I finally made my way to the edge, and I saw a man, watching me from behind, I couldn't see his face...but I swore it was him, with everything I was. No matter how many times I try to see his face, I only ever see my own. But I know it's him. Every night, I see. He wanted to show me something...

Beat.

...All those bodies, broken like old puppets before their master, as he stood there, I thought it would be me next in the pile. But no, I was special. I wouldn't be like him. To awake from such a nightmare and find myself here...it makes me question how deep a man's fantasy can really take him. Perhaps as far as he's willing to go.

ELLIOT: You're talking about Adam, aren't you?

Beat.

EDWARD: I was young, angry. He had murdered seven people, his last victim, a national treasure, a woman who had denied him in his career as a failed musician. In her chest, he carved two words, a name 'Adam Apocalypse' He was the celebrity of his time, a criminal mind that no-one could unlock. He was so curious to me...and I to him. In exchange for my time, he would tell me things, and I would tell those things for praise. Little did I know, I was merely a pawn, nothing to anyone. I did things...burned myself in his name. The world fell, and...I tried to make it right...but the world is unforgiving, and dark. One as drowned as I in his madness, requires something far stronger to drink than superstition and fear.

EDWARD exits, ELLIOT drinks from the well. She exits.

END OF ISSUE IV

MOVEMENT III ISSUE V

'Of Gods and Men'

Adam's mountain cave in The Madlands, the terror of our time enters, wheeling in his latest victim GODFEAR, bound to a chair, a pleasant hum, his victim blindfolded. He fetches a container filled with kerosene and a paintbrush, he fetches himself a stool, and sits. ADAM's thick sunglasses covering his eyes.

ADAM: Easy now, that's it. The worst is over and done with, you did it. I'm so proud.

ADAM dips the paintbrush in the bucket, smothering his victim in a foul-smelling liquid.

Relax, I'm going to clean you. Inside and out. You want to know what the biggest burden of them all is? People think it's choices, but no, oh no, you have control over your choices, you get to choose. No, it's options. That's what's scary. Before today, you had options, even when you had no choices. "Maybe he'll let me go." "Maybe someone will save me." Till finally, here and now, I have freed you of your options. I might have been the first honest man you've encountered on this side of the war. So, when I tell you that there is no help coming, that this is where your story ends, oh, you shouldn't be afraid. You should look me in the eye...

ADAM removes the blindfold.

...And thank me.

GODFEAR: What's that smell?

ADAM: Purification. Inevitable and holy.

GODFEAR begins to mumble a prayer to himself.

ADAM: What's that?

GODFEAR proceeds to mumble.

SPEAK UP!

GODFEAR: GOD HELP ME!

ADAM: ...That's the spirit. *(Calmly)* Father, I need to confess my sins.

GODFEAR: You expect me to listen?

ADAM: No, but it is expected of you, nonetheless. A condemned man who might confess the truth in a burning chapel, might have his secrets purged in the blaze. Therefore, he is safe to speak till come the ashes.

ADAM removes his glasses.

Look at me. Father, for so long I've been considered the great unscratchable itch of mankind. Do you know how that feels? To have them claw at you out of fear your entire adult life? We are but frail portraits in the end, all of us. Cruelly and crudely painted by the people who hate and despise us. I've tried for so long. And for all my hard work, this is my reward? To only have captivated the attention of a liar!? *This is how he repays me...*

The old had its time, don't you think? It was born in caves just like this across the world, its hopes were moulded by false gods, how pathetic. If there was even such a thing as God, he'd be a bigger 'madman' than I, and you'd all love him for it. The old had their time, and, they had the responsibility of keeping it. It was you who started it, not me. The world believes it was Eve who tempted Adam's hand to bite the apple, but no, it was man's nature that forced his hand, it was man's nature all along. *He was right...*

I am sick. Father. I am frightened and lost. My past has caught up with me. I know what I should do, but I am too afraid to do it.

131

ADAM places his hand upon GODFEAR.

Tell him, I still see the light. Tell him, I still see. There's still time to walk back, there's still time.

Two WORLD PAINTERS enter. ADAM quickly removes his hand from GODFEAR.

PAINTER: Everything to your satisfaction, master?

ADAM: Yes, yes, what news?

PAINTER: The Bounty Hunter has crossed into The Madlands.

Beat.

ADAM: I see. Then let us proceed as planned.

Beat.

ADAM: Was there something else?

PAINTER: What of your prisoner?

Beat.

ADAM: Throw him in the mist, shackle his feet to this ruined purgatory.

The WORLD PAINTERS remove GODFEAR, they exit. ADAM remains alone, before exiting.

END OF ISSUE V

MOVEMENT III ISSUE VI

'The Madlands'

The shrouded marshland consumed by mist and ancient secrets. A WORLD PAINTER emerges, hunched over, a sign reading 'The End Is Far'. ELLIOT enters alongside EDWARD. The PAINTER rocks back and forth.

ELLIOT: We're here. You should stay close... *(Sombre)* forgive me, I had forgotten.

Beat.

When we lost my sister, my father sent every last man he could find out here to find her. When I learned she had been taken, I came here alone, searching for the great 'Adam Apocalypse'.

EDWARD: Just a child? You were braver than most.

ELLIOT: I was stupid.

EDWARD: Did you ever find him?

ELLIOT: No. There's nothing out here but screams and ghosts. When I returned, alone, I think my father was surprised to see me, not happy, nor relieved. Just...surprised. He was never the same after mother.

EDWARD: How did she die?

Beat.

ELLIOT: She got sick.

EDWARD: Sick like your father?

Beat.

133

EDWARD: How long has he been addicted to heroin? Sorry, I couldn't help but notice. You could say I some experience-

ELLIOT: I don't think that's your business. Without him, this would be the world you know. Perhaps you'll speak about him with some respect.

EDWARD: Do you think silencing me, absolves him?

ELLIOT: No. I'm not deluded. I know what he is, and I know what I've done to let it fester.

Beat.

(Looking at PAINTER) Once he convinces them to do his bidding, the poor souls are outcast from their homes and families, and so they come to The Madlands to find their master. Those who are successful do not last very long, often sent on suicidal missions, those who are unworthy, or he has no use of…end up here.

ELLIOT approaches the PAINTER with a bottle of water.

Here, it's ok, take some of my water.

PAINTER: You are one of fire and ruin. Your soul is open like a bloody wound, but your direction is concluded, you have sipped from the well *(To Edward)* He has not…yet he wears the master's gaze. Why have you come?

ELLIOT: We have come to find your master.

Beat.

PAINTER: *(To Edward)* This one has been before. Long ago. He has been expecting you, the windmill turns the air around our heads, the prophecy unfolds…praise be to Adam…

ELLIOT: What prophecy?

PAINTER: He spoke of you... The Master. Said that you would come. The daughter who lies because she must. Forgive me.

Imminently, the sound of a monstrous wind roars as all semblance of light is extinguished. THE PAINTERS accost ELLIOT, dragging her away. EDWARD's fate is uncertain. When the wind at last dies and the light returns, nothing remains.

END OF ISSUE VI

MOVEMENT III ISSUE VII

'Adam Apocalypse'

Later, Adam's unholy cavern. ELLIOT is carried in by two WORLD PAINTERS, they bound her to a chair. ELLIOT stirs, ADAM emerges from the darkness.

ADAM: I know how it feels, my dear. To be abandoned. To be comprised of fragile glass. Awaiting the inevitable day, they all so carelessly shout you to shards of nothing. I see you are broken too. Then again, my sympathy is limited when you assist the proposition of my death. This has been a long time coming, you and I. Do you remember the night I took your father's eyes? You stood so softly at the edge of your bedroom door, I considered taking you for my own. After all, you were so committed to believing the lie that exists in my form. More committed than my own merry men...more committed than me, so it seems.

Beat.

You were more resistant than I was. I'm told; However, you did in fact drink the water. So, considering you are clearly led by fear, more so than ferocity. You should consider what I'm telling you, a great compliment. You're welcome, by the way.

ELLIOT: You think I care about the words of a man whose manipulated countless innocent people into turning on their own-

ADAM: THERE ARE NO INNOCENTS!

Beat.

Across the span of human history, despite technological innovation, unionisation through religious and political ideology and the so-called civilisation of the untamed world. The human race has time and time again proven itself incapable of change.

ADAM: In my time, at the height of man's technological movement, I offered them change in the form of music and song.

I offered them non-conformity to the great system of thievery, pain and deception. And I was silenced, mutilated, twisted into a story that I wanted no part of. When at last, the skies tore open with fire and death. The ground shook and wailed with defeat...I danced at the end of all things. Finally, the world in all its futility had come to an end. But then came your father...a sick man with a sick wife, who told the story of mankind's remission.

It is true, I have done all I can to prevent the tumour latching upon the canvas of creation, but, my dear, I do not appreciate being credited for work that is not mine.

Beat.

Your father is addicted to greed...amongst other vices. When your mother passed, he could not help but indulge. That must have been awful for you.

ELLIOT: Stop it.

ADAM: He sold her, didn't he? Your sister. Sold her body, heart and soul for a fix...but not President Death, oh no, how could Death be so predictable? You knew. But all the king's horses and all the king's men, were never in doubt they could mend the king's heart again...or something like that. I warned him of his deception, and I took his eyes. I will be sure to employ the most creative of endings for your father, when the time comes.

ELLIOT: Let me get out of this chair, I might help you brainstorm.

ADAM: We're counting on it.

EDWARD enters.

137

ELLIOT: What is this?

EDWARD: Quite funny, when you think about it. Look at her little face, she still doesn't understand.

ELLIOT: You're with him?

EDWARD: With him? No, you see, he's nothing. An echo. I mean, how should I explain this, so many ways, so much time, so much fun...I am the scream.

EDWARD screams manically.

Beat.

And he...is the whisper.

ELLIOT: I don't understand.

EDWARD: Sure, you do, I mean, how could you not? A poor little girl whose father glanced over her for all her life. There was a time where you would've done anything to be just like him. To wear his crown...but what is a paupers' crown but his name? My father deprived me of mine. He showed me what the world was, and like a red tide sweeping through the sky, I watched the world burn long before any of you would have to endure it.

Then I found a young man, full of ambition, care, and...delusion. Someone had to set him free, and where better to do such a thing but from the confines of a cell? I wear the skin of a tortured soul, but beneath...I am the architect of the damned, the voice in the dark that calls to the lost, I am the first, the last and the always. And...I am sorry, my dear, truly.

But you are far too important to be spared, far too adored. Your city will burn, and the people will tear down your father, frail and weak as he is. And when your monument to the damned is left in ruins...a new world will arise, for I, am your apocalypse. I am your salvation.

ELLIOT: If you kill me, my father will hunt you down like a dog. Whatever you think you know.

ADAM: Really? Your sick, blind, addict of a father? I can imagine him scrambling beneath a blanket without that doctor of yours.

ELLIOT attempts to wrestle free of the chair. Two WORLD PAINTERS enter, restraining her. ADAM is handed a small blade, he approaches ELLIOT. EDWARD watches from the distance.

EDWARD: WAIT! No, we bring her with us.

ADAM: Why?

EDWARD: She may yet prove useful; I am awfully fond of an ironic end. For the purposes of sating that indulgence in the interim; As she never spoke the truth about her father with her own lips, carve out her tongue.

ELLIOT struggles.

Ooh, feisty and fiery! Dancing with her tongue as if it were a sword of burning righteousness. Beautiful, the contours, the fear, the rage…what would a dragon be without her wings? I shall remake you in my own image. *As the world did for me…*

ELLIOT: Get your hands off me, I swear to God, I will rip your fucking hearts out!

ADAM cuts ELLIOT's tongue from her mouth, blood pisses everywhere. she is unbound and left on the floor, unable to speak, only whimper. ADAM lowers to ELLIOT's level.

ADAM: Do not despair, my dear. I see greatness in you, as the master saw greatness in me. In such darkness as this, you are as much of Adam as I. To prove my love for you, and to seal our bond. I will eat your words as if they were my own.

139

ADAM eats ELLIOT's tongue.

EDWARD: Your father sent you here to die, now, together we shall return, to live. To build a new world, free of the past. Don't fret, this is all just a dream...one as old as time itself, a story told well, becomes the truth, even if it is a lie. Bring the girl to the chamber.

The WORLD PAINTERS drag ELLIOT away, they exit.

ADAM: *(To Edward)* You are playing a dangerous game.

EDWARD: It is my game to play. I should hope you would remember that after the last time you and your little puppets thought about dancing off of their strings. Don't lose yourself, you have been enjoying the mantle of my name far too much. Should I be concerned?

Beat.

ADAM: No.

EDWARD: Good. Ensure she is ready in time, tomorrow, a new world arises, and it must be by her hand. Do not fail me, or I will find another who won't. You still belong to me, everything you are. Edward.

ADAM drops to his knees, clutching his head.

You are still not worthy of the name. Do you understand me? You are a puppet, nothing more. How dare you mock me with even the suggestion you could wear what my father was prized apart from? Now, tell me your name.

EDWARD slaps ADAM across the face, hard.

ADAM: I am nothing, my privilege is your will. I am Adam, I am Adam.

END OF ISSUE VII

MOVEMENT III ISSUE VIII

'The Truth'

A video projection plays upon the stage, somewhere in a barren, dimly lit room. ADAM and EDWARD are opposite one another.

ADAM: Let me go.

EDWARD: Excuse me?

ADAM: Why won't you let me go?

EDWARD: Did you let me go?

Beat.

Besides, where would you go? You'd struggle against the tide, your arms would grow restless, you are only safe in here, with me.

ADAM: Give me my name.

EDWARD: It has already been given.

ADAM: Please.

EDWARD: Does a plead ever release a man from a terrible dream? As a boy I suffered intensely with sleep apnoea, unable to move, unable to breath. I imagined myself drowning, terrified, with only a fantasy to comfort me. When I succumbed, I was traumatised, but was permitted to awaken once more. We are not who we think we are, Adam. You now know this better than any man living, yet like me, they have made you silent. But I shall give you... VOICE!

The projection dies.

END OF ISSUE VIII

141

DEATH: What news?

Beat.

Is he dead?

Beat.

My daughter, is she dead?

Beat.

Are **you** dead? Speak!

PAINTER: Your daughter is alive-

DEATH: Damn her, what about Adam!?

PAINTER: The Bounty Hunter brought him, bound by rope.

DEATH: Very good, send him in. I expect he'll desire quick payment.

PAINTER: It's not that simple, your grace. Ropes also bind your daughter. And, you are aware that your people are amassing outside the city gates?

DEATH: Their treachery will be dealt with soon enough, I assure you. Any news of my Doctor? My...I need...where is he!?

PAINTER: There is still no sign of him, my king. There have been a small number of incidents against the palace guard. Perhaps we should consider evacuating you and your daughter from the city?

DEATH glares at the PAINTER.

I will bring them at once.

PAINTER exits.

EDWARD enters, behind him, ADAM is bound by rope, behind him, ELLIOT, her mouth bandaged in a similar fashion to her father's eyes. Behind him, trails the PAINTER.

EDWARD: I have returned, Death Merchant.

DEATH: Let me hear his voice.

ADAM approaches DEATH.

ADAM: Do I still speak so softly in your ear, my king?

DEATH: Guards! Guards! Throw him in a cell! Throw that demon into the darkest pit you can find!

Two WORLD PAINTERS enter, they escort ADAM away, exiting.

DEATH: You have fulfilled your end of the bargain, 'Pacifist', now I will fulfil mine.

EDWARD: Your victory has cost you dearly. Your city. Your daughter. A pity I couldn't save her for you.

DEATH: Bring her closer to me.

EDWARD brings ELLIOT before her father; He softly strokes her face.

She is no daughter of mine.

ELLIOT reaches out against her father, EDWARD and the last PAINTER carry her away, exiting. DEATH remains ill upon his throne. Atop a lonely box, stands GODFEAR. He cries out to an assembly of WORLD PAINTERS.

GODFEAR: Here we stand! People of New Albion! Discontent! Starved of justice! I have journeyed to the gates of hell; I have seen the darkness that will swallow us bloody! Our leader is a fool! He is weak! He has brought a plague down upon our people! But I have seen a knight in that darkness, a man they call 'The Pacifist'

He saved me when I was left for dead! And he asked me to come to you, the people, and tell you of what I saw. We must band together, for only together, can we build a faithful world, a just world. Death cares not for the faithful nor the just! Banished his own mad daughter to a dark cell, so they say! If our leader will not lead us! Then we shall lead ourselves in the lord's name! To war! To ruin! And the world's ending!

GODFEAR offers a chalice, filled with an unholy water, he serves Adam now. In a ritual to the tune of 'Mars, the bringer of War' by Gustav Holst, the WORLD PAINTERS drink and become rabid, as EDWARD watches from the distance, drinking from a plastic bottle, laughing to himself. Eventually the PAINTERS charge off into the dark. Followed by GODFEAR. A WORLD PAINTER enters, and approaches DEATH.

PAINTER: Sire! The world is burning! Your people storm the city gates, our men are overwhelmed. The cultists have rallied a mob to their cause, we tried to despatch them, but they are intertwined with too many of our own to tell the mad from the many. What are your orders?

DEATH: Insolent rats. Traitorous dogs. Mayflies with devil's horns! Madness at the gates! Madness in their hearts! Kill them all.

PAINTER: Sire...you cannot-

DEATH: I am their king, their president, and their master. You will command their destruction on my behalf.

PAINTER: Sire.

145

The PAINTER exits. DEATH remains upon his throne, he fetches a sword, he awaits destruction. We move to a dark cell, somewhere beneath the palace. ADAM is thrown by WORLD PAINTERS into the black, he laughs to himself as he falls, beside him, in an adjoining cell, ELLIOT. The sound of battling in the distance.

ADAM: Do you hear that, my dear? Hidden within the survival instinct of man is his doom. Your father chooses to fight. I know, my dear. He took your voice long ago, robbed you of your right to life. And when faced with you, an embarrassment to him. He casts you away. Fear not, my child. For I care for you, for I shall let you speak once more.

ADAM approaches ELLIOT, she resists.

Do not fight, good child, sweet child. You and I are as one.

ADAM cradles ELLIOT, he removes her mouth coverings.

Speak your heart, and I will listen.

ELLIOT discovers she is able to speak, however in reality, she only believes she can as ADAM humours her, no-one else can understand her.

ELLIOT: I am broken…I am lost. I am falling, with not even the cold earth to catch me.

ADAM: Then I shall catch you.

ELLIOT: You can hear me?

ADAM: I can hear you.

ELLIOT: He did this to me. Sent me to die.

ADAM: He did.

ELLIOT: I will make him pay; I will cut his tongue from his mouth. He betrayed me.

ADAM: He did.

Two WORLD PAINTERS enter alongside EDWARD, ADAM nods to his master, who permits him to order the PAINTERS to untie them both.

(To Elliot) Strike your knife into him, then join us on the docks. Together, we shall build a new world.

ELLIOT exits.

We have the ship?

EDWARD: We do. You must take our people there and leave at once.

ADAM: Leave?

EDWARD: I cannot go with you, not if our plan is to succeed. You no longer need me, Adam.

Beat.

Go. The work is done. Lead our people across the ocean, to a brave new world.

ADAM: Thank you, master.

ADAM exits, followed by EDWARD.

END OF ISSUE IX

MOVEMENT III ISSUE X

'The End of The World'

The sound of a battle rages. ELLIOT enters, she dances around as her father with a blade, DEATH, attempts to protect himself. The audience are able to understand ELLIOT, but her father cannot.

ELLIOT: My whole life, you've done nothing but think about yourself.

DEATH: Daughter? Is that you, just...please, let me explain.

ELLIOT: You've ruined me, let the world tear me apart. You never cared about me.

DEATH: Elliot, please. Let's be reasonable and just talk about this.

ELLIOT: You're not even listening to me now, are you? You never listen!

DEATH: I can't understand what you're saying, Elliot, please.

ELLIOT: Liar!

ELLIOT charges into her father, DEATH struggles against ELLIOT as she plunges the blade into him, multiple times. EDWARD enters alongside GODFEAR and a WORLD PAINTER.

EDWARD: Stop her!

The PAINTER tackles ELLIOT to the ground, she's rabid.

GODFEAR: She's mad!

EDWARD: They both are.

148

GODFEAR assists the PAINTER in restraining ELLIOT.

Guard, we must act quickly to bring order back to the city.

PAINTER: What should we do?

EDWARD: The boat leaving the harbour, you must sink it.

PAINTER: But, without the ship, how will we-

EDWARD: Listen to me, Adam's cult is aboard that boat, this may be our only chance to stop him. Be on the right side of history, my friend. Sink them to the depths of the sea.

PAINTER: Very well.

PAINTER exits.

GODFEAR: *(To Edward)* You are a true hero, sir. I will be sure to tell your story to every person I find. You are the one to lead us into the future, after this, the people will be looking to someone to protect them.

EDWARD: Well, I will do whatever I can. I'll keep an eye on her. Go on, you have people who need you. And Godfear?

Beat.

...I'm glad you found him first.

EDWARD approaches ELLIOT, she cowers in fear.

No, no, this isn't right. Is this all it ever took? Some simple trick, one man with the sum of his words!? Is that all it ever took to unravel you people!? No, it's too easy...too simple, it can't be done, I can't have won. No, there's more, more, there's always more. Unless...I have only unravelled myself. Could something so real be a dream? Once upon a time, I endured many fantasies in fire, yet...

EDWARD grips her face tightly.

...This one feels so real. Perhaps I will cut you...for what bleeds, can't lie. Don't fret my dear, I suspect that you and I shall become very fine friends indeed.

The radio returns.

COLIN: Our king and master, Edward Cross, was appointed by a unanimous decision of the populace of the capital, to become the president, master, king and...oh, why can't there just be one title? It's been a wild turn of events, Brian.

BRIAN: And yet, nothing has changed.

COLIN: Adam Apocalypse is dead, his cult too. The Death Merchant is overthrown, his daughter, maddened and tortured. Not to mention we have a new High Chancellor of The New Ancient Apostles and a new man on the throne of Manning Station.

BRIAN: And yet, nothing has changed.

COLIN: It's been three days.

BRIAN: Till tomorrow. Besides, I'm not convinced.

COLIN: You never are. Are you?

BRIAN: Who told you that Adam Apocalypse was really on that boat?

COLIN: Oh, Jesus Christ.

BRIAN: All I'm saying is, Colin...don't you find it strange that one man, with no serious armament, ventures into the most dangerous territory in New Albion, faces an entire cult including their leader, all by himself.

BRIAN: Then, this man apprehends said cult leader, rescues both a damsel and a priest, marches into a city that just so happens to be in the midst of a well-timed revolution. And then, within three days, establishes himself as the most powerful man in the region, and somehow anyone who could be called as a witness to these events is either dead or paid for? Doesn't that seem...strange?

COLIN: Maybe he just has a way with words.

Beat.

BRIAN: ...Yeah, you're probably right.

The radio dies.

END OF ISSUE X

NOTES ON MOVEMENT III CHAPTER II

Cannot be performed independently of Chapter I, without written permission from Animated Assembly Theatre Company.

Intended Performance Style: Expressionistic. Physical. Performative. Loud. Animated. Emotive.

Intended Mise-En-Scene: Decadent. Surrealistic. Psychological. Dystopian. Doomed. Bleak. Insane. Damned.

In this conclusion to the work, regret takes hold. The ideology of Adam is dead. With Edward now crowned king; His character has devolved significantly. His intelligence and ferocity have somewhat diminished as he has embraced his new identity. It is a metaphor for how power pacifies potential. We require struggle to thrive, as much as most would hate to admit it. Having achieved his victory in Chapter 1, Adam Everyman now begins to question the validity of his reality, having believed he was merely asleep, he indulged the fantasy as best he could, much like he did in Movement I, yet the dream is unending.

A direct confrontation between two narratives spills itself across Edward's mind. In one, he is a madman turned king, risking the alienation of his own people, prompting a seemingly inevitable destruction. And in another reality, he is trapped in a nightmare without end, and once a vision of his magnum opus 'Adam Apocalypse' greets him, the true Adam realises the only way to escape is to take his own life.

Adam begins to panic, attempting to dance between the worst of both worlds as his kingdom collapses around him. Adam contemplates his own destruction in an isolated setting, mirroring the events of Movement II to some degree.

Ultimately, this movement discusses the question "What becomes of us if we are trapped in a reality that we cannot accept?" Which I would argue is the quintessential question of the entire work. The process of finding truth amidst contradiction, bias, foolishness and emotion. The music of mankind is chaos.

CHARACTERS

EDWARD: Middle aged, Adam Everyman's alter ego. When Ideology dies, and fantasy falters, this is all that remains. A King of Nothing.

APOCALYPSE: Middle aged, what would appear to be 'Adam Apocalypse' having survived his master's betrayal in Chapter 1. The true Edward.

GODFEAR: Middle-aged, appointed a powerful position, Godfear is a man of morals, tested against a waning manipulator who attempts to control his every move.

ELLIOT: Late-Twenties, known as 'The Creature', a hollow shell of a once powerful woman.

ANTON YELLOWFEVER: Middle-aged, the junior adjutant for The New Albion Guard.

FORDIO GLAMIS: Late twenties, The most popular man alive.

THE SYMPHONY OF ADAM APOCALYPSE

MOVEMENT THREE

CHAPTER II

'Regret'

MOVEMENT III ISSUE XI

'Throne of Tomorrow'

2074. The throne room of a once idealistic king of New Albion, a monument to mankind's odyssey in the New Ancient World. EDWARD sits upon his throne, dead eyed, where once existed vibrancy of thought and action, now exists fatigue, the dystopian world of Movement III is changing, madness, seeks its slumber. GODFEAR enters alongside a PAINTER, who carries a wooden box, wrapped in chains and cloth.

GODFEAR: All hail King Edward! Valiant president, embodiment of mastery...lord and protector of New Albion and all her-

EDWARD: Yes, yes. Godfear, you may dispense with the wretched formalities. What do you want?

GODFEAR: I bring troubling news from The Madlands, and...a gift.

GODFEAR nods to the PAINTER, who places the box down, unwrapping it.

EDWARD: What is this?

GODFEAR reveals a key which he sets down upon the box.

GODFEAR: A young man rode to the city walls this morning, rabid with reason. He was screaming of a pain inside his bones, the feeling of a thousand shards of glass removing themselves from his mind. At first, we believed him to have been one of the lost cultists, still wandering the barren marshes of the Madlands in search of their master. I and two of my congregation endeavoured to take him to one of the ancient wells, hoping that the unholy water would alleviate him with the sensation of his master's presence. When at last we arrived, we were dismayed, the shroud of the Madlands has all but dissipated. Before us, lay the sight of hundreds of dead creatures and lost cultists. It seems this sight has all but confirmed what the missionaries have told us. An ill omen makes its way south.

EDWARD: What happened to the young man?

GODFEAR: Death. Forgive me, I imagine you'd have wished to speak with him yourself, unfortunately, for reasons we can't explain, he did not survive more than a few hours in our care. There were no physical wounds, no signs of foul play on the body...

Silence as GODFEAR approaches his king.

My president and king, my master and merchant. There is something far larger at work. Settlements are falling silent. The old perish, while the young are taking a strange turn. They are...Gathering, articulating strange ideas that defy your doctrine of unity. Our armies to the north have since reported heavy losses, not by the hands of any enemy, but by some invisible killer, the likes of which has never been seen. At first, we suspected a plague, but...

Beat.

EDWARD: ...What is the mood of the people on this matter?

GODFEAR: Panic, unruly, maddening panic. There are those, wild eyed, foaming at the mouth who proclaim you... guilty of a politician's flaws, they raise their fingers to your statues and proclaim your iron fist... rusted, and unfit for purpose. As they once did before to your predecessor.

EDWARD: What is it with you people? All I have done in my time is try to save you from yourselves, I've played your games, your politics...I've...what more could I possibly do? What does the church have to say on this matter?

Silence.

Godfear?

GODFEAR: Many have turned from our faith. There have been... false rumours claiming the church is now merely an extension of your government, a tool to quell any further uprisings since... the last one.

EDWARD: Our armies are stretched as thin as it is, who else should keep the people on their leash? A Gretchling!? These dissidents... do you know where they've gone? These 'Never-Believers'

GODFEAR: Yes.

EDWARD: Then bring me a platter of their treacherous tongues.

Beat.

GODFEAR: But...my king, is that not an act of provocation on our part? We wouldn't want to inspire chaos, would we?

EDWARD: Let me make something abundantly clear, Godfear. And perhaps you can enlighten the population of a memory that they have too soon forgotten. 'Adam Apocalypse' is dead. I killed him, I killed them all...do you understand?

GODFEAR: I have defied legend and legacy both. And if anyone, from The Southern Shit Knife to The Northern Wastes, wishes to challenge that fact. I will celebrate the past... WITH THEIR BLOOD!

EDWARD slams his hand down, calling out...

ANTON! GET IN HERE!

ANTON YELLOWFEVER enters, an inexperienced, easily manipulated man.

ANTON: You summoned me, my leader.

EDWARD: Behold, Godfear...the perfect New Albion soldier. Loyal, competent, with his mind and heart commanded by his country, not his own need to satiate lower human desires. Anton...where do your allegiances lay?

ANTON: With you, lord and master. With your will, for which I pledge unwavering conviction.

EDWARD: You see, Godfear, every soldier in our army understands that in order to avoid the chaos of the past, we must unite in one thought, one moment with one heart. I will hear no more of suspicions concerning rumours propagated by our enemies. No, the conquest to the north has been assured to me by The High Commander to be well underway. However, in his absence, it seems I am left without those strong willed enough to see a new world born out of the old...Anton Yellowfever?

ANTON: My king?

EDWARD: I name you acting 'High Commander' of New Albion, till your predecessor returns. Serve me with excellence, and you will be rewarded. Plague me with your own reason, and I will permit you eternal darkness, do I make myself clear?

ANTON: I am honoured, my protector. What would you command of me?

157

EDWARD: Prepare a small force to begin searching the hills, the settlements, all over...issue a bounty to the local guilds; Treasures for the tongues of traitors.

ANTON: As you command.

ANTON exits.

GODFEAR: What of the Madlands?

EDWARD: No, what of Fordio Glamis?

GODFEAR: A man with a voice, nothing more.

EDWARD: So was I, once.

Beat.

I wish to know the content of these little speeches he provides to the masses; I suggest you-

GODFEAR: Forgive my interruption this one time in a decade, but I think the pressing matter is that of The Madlands!

EDWARD: WHAT OF THEM!? They are lands, empty...the weather does not concern me, the thoughts of the rat populace concern me! You expect me to sit here and embrace these people, is that it? If in twenty years, mankind believes one Armageddon permits return to our futility, I shall stamp out their beliefs and carve out their brains, and serve them to a host of wild DOGS! I want them found! And I want no more rumours of oddities in the world. The only disease is that which travels the tongues of traitors. I am tired of this debate.

GODFEAR: And with the soldiers in the north? What if the stories are true?

EDWARD: ...Then the realm will grieve in my favour. And New Albion will be as silent as a strong host awaiting a powerful enemy.

158

GODFEAR: You are playing a dangerous game.

EDWARD: It is not my game, but yours.

Beat.

I've tried for too long to settle around the hypocrisies of men, thinking I could stare the bull down with my eyes and will alone. No, the only way to survive locking horns with such a devastating animal as man, is to ride him into the ground, stab him in the side a thousand times over. I can only change things through the means that the people allow me, Godfear. I have tried patience, now I will try peace...at any expense.

GODFEAR: Sire, protector... if we silence the many...do we not risk their unity against us?

EDWARD: If we do not...do they not risk my wrath? We are saving the people, Godfear, from my terror, brutal and unwavering as ever. Suggest to the masses, they take great care in their next move.

Silence.

What else is there?

GODFEAR: From the Madlands... *(Indicating the box)* A patrol ventured to a shrouded cave; Its entrance marked by two posts, adorned in red blood fabric...it is merely an oddity, a relic. Nothing more.

EDWARD: Yes, well, I think that'll be enough surprises for today, Godfear. On your way.

GODFEAR bows, he, and the PAINTER exit.

END OF ISSUE XI

MOVEMENT III ISSUE XII

'The Torment of Yesterday'

EDWARD *sits upon his throne, his knee bouncing, he looks towards the box, approaching it.*

EDWARD: Insolence. Even in a delusion. What trickery is this? What plots do dead men speak from yesterday? Mocking my eyes with thorns...with whispers on the wind, of so-called 'reason'. How did it come to this? Why still does the great game go on and on? Fools! I gave them 'Adam Apocalypse'. I gave them unity; I gave them reason. Now they use their tongues against me? THEM!? They dare to lick the soles of my feet as starving dogs with waning loyalty... I WILL USHER IN A SECOND GREAT CALAMITY BEFORE I ENTERTAIN SUCH MADNESS!

EDWARD *opens the box, revealing inside, the puppet from Movement I. He backs away, frightened, leaning against his throne.*

THE TORMENT OF A CHILD!

PAINTER: *(Offstage)* Glorious Leader, does something trouble you?

EDWARD: OUT! LEAVE ME IN SILENCE! I HAVE THOUGHTS OF DREAMS FAR BEYOND YOUR UNDERSTANDING! GET AWAY!

In darkness, a familiar voice emerges.

APOCALYPSE: ...Even in this late hour, see how the merchant of madness cowers.

EDWARD: ...That voice...I don't believe it. Show yourself!

APOCALYPSE *emerges, his thick retro aviators broken, his clothing torn and soaked with water.*

160

APOCALYPSE: There is much more than a world in the water... my 'King'... would you care to see it?

EDWARD: Impossible.

APOCALYPSE: You disposed of me like a mongrel dog without a second passing thought...poor 'King' sad 'King' sorry 'King'... How soon did the fantasy of your brave new world begin to decay before they began to drool in your presence?

EDWARD: The fantasy...is not over. I still hold my throne, you are but a ghost of the past, nothing more. All of this...is under my control, IN MY MIND! NOT YOURS!

APOCALYPSE: Is that because the idea of me being real, is too terrifying even for you to bear?

EDWARD: What is it you want? Your name! I give it to you, 'Edward' now go!

APOCALYPSE: I am neither your Edward, nor your Adam...I am all you have left me to be.

EDWARD: *(Indicating the puppet)* How did you come by this?

APOCALYPSE: Of all your distant dreams of other worlds, how fitting it is that your own victory determines your paralysis. The day was won, and the world was yours, yet still, you sleep...even as a dismal dream dies. There are two answers, old friend. In one world, I survived and scavenged him from the ruins of a household not far from here. How fitting your father's work and your own should confront you before the end. The two tragedies of two puppeteers, playing as Gods among men. Of course, there is another way, the prospect this is all just a delusion...another night terror, for a world so wild and a victory that came so easy must be more unlikely than the sight before you now. I suppose it is a question of "What do you believe?"

161

EDWARD: You don't think I've tried to awaken!? The game was won, it was OVER! We are still there, you and I, in our game...Edward, in a world sick and hollow. This throne...its feeling is so rough, imperfect. My body is tired, it aches and grows weary...time is without meaning or mercy. There are no fountains of gold, no green. There's nothing. If this is truly a dream, then why have you come? *(Hopeful)* Perhaps you herald my wake?

APOCALYPSE lifts the puppet.

APOCALYPSE: The strings of your reign are snapping under the weight of your sins and the laws of men and science have already condemned your fall. All you have is time. I have come to warn you...there are those in New Albion, those in this very palace who devour fantasies of their own. I will come to you two more times. In order for you to survive, you will have to decide what is real and what is of your own conjuring. The world you've created, or the world you've sought to destroy all your life. How does your symphony end? Good king? By Adam's hand or by Edward's?

APOCALYPSE exits.

END OF ISSUE XII

MOVEMENT III ISSUE XIII

'The one who says nothing, tells all'

EDWARD slams his hands down upon the arms of his throne, pacing the floor. The PAINTER returns, alongside them, ELLIOT, a muted woman with bandages across the entirety of her face, scars and stains of dirt across her body, chains which reach down to the floor bound to her malnourished wrists.

PAINTER: The creature...as you requested.

EDWARD: Leave us.

PAINTER: Sire...with all due respect, is that truly wise?

EDWARD: Perhaps not, but it is a necessity that you do so to keep a consistent relationship between your neck and your head. Go.

Beat.

PAINTER: ...Very good, my lord and master.

PAINTER exits.

EDWARD inspects ELLIOT.

EDWARD: Look at you... screaming in silence. The sins of the father do tell tales in the eyes of the daughter. Is there something you would tell me? If you had a tongue. It must be painful for you, truly...to have so much to say, to have known you had so much potential...and all of it...for dust. If Godfear was truly devoted to his puppeteer, he would carve out his own tongue. There is no greater trust in confession, than to speak with one who is eternally silent. There in which lays...the great lure of the lie.

EDWARD: You have long wished to kill me. It is in your blood, commanded by your blood. Your father was monstrous, yet, even though you plunged the knife in his back as the city fell...I am the orchestrator of the damned, the player of evil, in your mind. All I wanted...was for you to see. To make you as beautiful to me as Adam was, for a moment. You doubt I ever believed? I have never believed more.

 Even now, the world, as grim and hollow as it is, seeks to return to the conditions that led us into this great calamity, don't they understand!? If we return, it is as if we are resetting the clock. It ticks away, and those who hear it...the sound is maddening, tick, tick, tick, tick...the tortuous sound of the symphony. All I wanted was for someone to share in an idea, that the sound was real, and the pain of it was deafening, I did all I could to make them see...and they would not listen to one man, I GAVE THEM AN IDEA! And still...they resisted.

Now I smell plots to the left and right of my throne, a cold shadow on my back, wandering eyes...yet with you...I sense nothing. Could you understand? After all these years? I tried... I know you don't believe me, but I have tried to bring them into a new world, to step away from the past...yet they cling to their books and memories and stories over burning fires, how sadistic is the intelligent man!

Someone means to kill me. I can sense it...as did the merchant of death. He sat upon this throne and drowned in his paranoia. And I...regarded him as a dancing fool and nothing more, yet...what if he knew what I did not? What if this station, this throne of tomorrow...what if it heralds ambition? Chaos gives cause for the human condition to exist beyond limitation. When people are given permission to think, and time to act...every man, woman, and child, will become obsessed with power before long.

Where is the snake in the jungle?

END OF ISSUE XIII

MOVEMENT III ISSUE XIV

'To Catch a Traitor'

GODFEAR enters alongside a PAINTER.

GODFEAR: ...What is she doing here?

EDWARD: That does not concern you, Godfear. What news?

GODFEAR: What news? You rally the city guard, the people come to their church in fear...surely, I should ask this question of you?

EDWARD: I do not appreciate your tone. You would be wise to remember your position. Perhaps another walk of atonement would stain your feet with some humility?

GODFEAR: If is your will, so be it. But tell me, why have you rallied the guard?

Beat.

EDWARD: ...Does their presence interfere with plans of yours, Godfear?

GODFEAR: ...I only wish to know what I must tell the people.

EDWARD: And I shall tell you, but first, bring me Anton and Fordio. Then we will speak of tellings and tales.

GODFEAR: For what purpose?

EDWARD: I can imagine you will find out, now go.

GODFEAR: Very well, should we begin to make preparations in the event-

EDWARD: If I wanted preparations to be made, you can be damn well sure that I'd do it myself.

Silence.

Go.

GODFEAR and the PAINTER exit.

EDWARD: *(To Elliot)* Did you see? A question…a tone…no doubt next shall be a criticism.

END OF ISSUE XIV

MOVEMENT IV ISSUE XV

'Veni, Vidi, Vici'

APOCALYPSE emerges from the darkness, silent and still.

EDWARD: *(To Elliot)* Tell me you see him...TELL ME!

APOCALYPSE: And thus, the flaw in your massacre of mouths shows itself to be true. When no-one can speak, there is little distinction between fiction and fearful truth. A secure man would summon his guards...but no, you've silenced the world in your delusional paranoia.

EDWARD: Delusional?

APOCALYPSE: Delusional. Your mind is butchered like a wild pig...cut up savagely with silver words.

EDWARD: You dare?

APOCALYPSE: You did.

EDWARD: You are nothing but a ghost, a shadow of a thought...a piece of tin foil performing ballet across my own mouth, threatening to cause me pain when you should stumble upon my fillings.

APOCALYPSE: If you truly believe that...then why do you fear me?

EDWARD: Fear you?

Beat.

EDWARD reaches for the puppet; He begins to pull it apart.

I DO NOT FEAR YOU! I MADE YOU! AND, AS I PUT YOU TOGETHER, I WILL UNMAKE YOU! YOU ARE AN IDEA!

APOCALYPSE: Tell me, if your music, your ideas…if all of it was so worth the cost of sanity…why now when you have won, and the lie of your name and story is maintained…do you have nothing at all?

APOCALYPSE exits.

EDWARD: BE GONE! YOU MAD FOOL!

GODFEAR, ANTON and FORDIO enter, watching EDWARD scream at the darkness.

RUN! RUN LIKE A WILD BEAST! WE SHALL SEE WHO WINS!

EDWARD turns.

END OF ISSUE XV

MOVEMENT III ISSUE XVI

'Game of Society'

GODFEAR: I have brought the men as you requested, sire.

ANTON: …Your grace.

FORDIO: …President and Master.

EDWARD: Gentleman…it is of grave importance that we speak.

GODFEAR: So it seems.

Silence.

EDWARD: Anton…what is the state of our military forces in the kingdom?

ANTON: With Commander Ghast engaged with the bulk of our forces in the wild lands to the north, we are, somewhat…stretched. Is there a threat, my king?

EDWARD: Yes, but it is a threat, the like of which, does not require the strength of arms alone, but the loyalty of responsible men. Are you a responsible man, Yellowfever?

ANTON: Of course, your valiant grace.

EDWARD: And, are you loyal?

ANTON: Command me in all things, sire. And it will be done.

Beat.

EDWARD: Good…and what of you? A so-called 'man of the people'. Fordio Glamis…do the people trust your word?

FORDIO: They do.

EDWARD: And, do you trust mine?

Silence.

FORDIO: Of course.

EDWARD: There comes a time where loyalty must surpass good words. Anton? Would you wish to prove your loyalty to me?

ANTON: Yes, your grace.

EDWARD: Order your men to seize this 'man of the people' have him skinned alive, his entrails splayed out, and have him decorate the palace walls.

FORDIO: ...My king?

EDWARD: I am sorry, Fordio, but there is only room for one 'man of the people' and it certainly isn't you. Commander Anton?

ANTON: Guard!?

GODFEAR: ...My king, if I may-

EDWARD: Do not make me question your position too, Godfear. I am merely removing a distraction from my sight, then we can begin to attend to the threat of our time.

FORDIO: Have me exiled into the Madlands, I'll leave the city and never return, you have my word!

EDWARD: YOUR WORD!? I HAVE THE WORDS OF A MAN WHO TALKS TO PLEASE THE PEOPLE! SHOULD THE PEOPLE TURN ON ME, INEVITABLY YOU MUST DO SO TO NOT LOSE POWER! SILENCE THIS DOG AT ONCE!

A PAINTER enters, FORDIO is escorted away.

FORDIO: YOU CAN'T DO THIS! THE PEOPLE WILL NOT ALLOW IT! DO YOU HEAR ME!? THE PEOPLE WILL NOT ALLOW IT!

FORDIO and the PAINTER exit.

GODFEAR: Might I speak candidly?

EDWARD: Let us see.

GODFEAR: What threat do you envision exists within the minds of the people? What great enemy causes you to execute the man who consoles them?

EDWARD: Incompetence, Godfear. I am streamlining the command structure of this kingdom.

GODFEAR: With barbarity?

EDWARD: With an opposition to so-called reasonable ideals that will lead us towards the anarchy of the past. It is only through chaotic contradiction that the world will never be thrown into a great calamity again.

GODFEAR: Because we will be forever in one!

Beat.

EDWARD: Your loyalty erodes with each passing moment, Godfear. I pray you do not fall ill to this disease; We would both hate for you to reap the consequences of such a thing. Gentleman, there is a threat…it is not yet aware of itself, but I have become aware of it. A permanent solution is available to us, but one that is drastic and will require great courage…we must move quickly to combat this so-called 'disease of reason' Commander Anton? How soon could you distribute your forces across every settlement within our borders?

ANTON: …Three days, perhaps two.

171

EDWARD: Good.

GODFEAR: For what purpose?

EDWARD: ...Reason thrives upon the people's ability to speak. It assists them in forming consensus, and consensus, is a dangerous enemy when it opposes you. Therefore, we shall remake the world to ensure that 'consensus' is all but a forgotten ideal. Commander Anton will therefore order his men to remove the tongues of every man, woman and child in New Albion. Those who resist with force, shall have their arms removed. Those who flee, their legs. Those who taunt, their eyes. We shall pluck the features of conspiracy and quell the old ways once and for all.

GODFEAR: There will be civil war.

EDWARD: Which is why we shall deploy our armies upon our own people. And you, loyal Godfear, will send your missionaries across the land to seize every source of food and water from every settlement in the kingdom. If a populace resists, it shall be starved. if it resists further...it shall be wiped off the face of the earth with fire and ruin. Do I make myself clear?

Beat.

GODFEAR: ...What has brought these ideas to your mind? This is wrong. Many of the soldiers will refuse the order. Commander! Speak for yourself, damn you! Tell him!

ANTON: It is...a possibility.

EDWARD: If the people turn, the realm will fall. Either way, we shall not return to the old ways. Not while I sit in this throne.

GODFEAR: ...As you wish.

GODFEAR bows and exits.

172

ANTON bows.

EDWARD: One more thing, commander...once our forces are in place and you have control over all of the water and food. Instruct your men to eliminate all of the missionaries. Is that understood?

ANTON: The entire church?

EDWARD approaches ANTON. Placing a hand on his shoulder.

EDWARD: ...There is no church.

ANTON bows and exits.

END OF ISSUE XVI

MOVEMENT III ISSUE XVII

'Suicide of The Symphony'

EDWARD returns to the empty throne. He speaks to ELLIOT.

EDWARD: Desperate times force our hand. To think that a global Armageddon alone is not enough to stay the hand that reaches for the hammer to rebuild the broken. They call me a hypocrite, as if they know better. They claim I brainwash; I claim they are brainwashed by fear to believe in the invisible and the eternal. They claim I am violent. For creatures who spend so much time looking into the past...they do have a selective memory for their own history. For thousands of years...the human story is one filled with bloodshed, yet children play at the hilarious, believing thousands of years might be altered in just one lifetime. Their lifetime. Because the young always demand noted attendance, with the exclusion of accountability. Man has always been mad. And the very idea that they should turn on me...

ME!? Perhaps it is the curse of my regal name...to meet this unfortunate end. For when I was with Adam, I was one with ambition and I knew flight. Now, I am less civilised...I shall churn their betrayal into the butter for my bread.

APOCALYPSE enters, he says nothing.

I DO NOT FEAR YOU NOR ANY MAN OR WOMAN! I HAVE ARMIES! AND WILL. SHEER BURNING WILL! AND I WILL PLUCK THE FEATURES FROM THE PEOPLE, ONE BY ONE, GENERATION BY GENERATION TILL I AM CONFIDENT THAT I SHALL NEVER HAVE TO ENDURE THEIR WORLD AGAIN! You speak of an eternal fate...I understood, it was the people, they would turn, and I would become yesterday, because I know the truth...the fantasy endures. This is all for me! But I am not going to falter, I will not awake to what you or anyone else believes the world to be, I will sit in this throne and-

174

Silence.

EDWARD: …You…have tricked me. I believed Godfear…the people, they would turn the gun on me, but no, they merely loaded it…I have killed myself. By my own hand…my own mind.

EDWARD begins to laugh hysterically. The sound of an air raid warning and fighting out on the streets outside.

I understand now. I see it…this is but a fantasy. I am asleep, my eyes shut, my mind elsewhere. The people are not returning to their ways, I am returning to theirs…I will awake, and begin again, begin anew. After all these years of wondering…It's another movement…another dance…nothing more. No truth, no sensibility…the world…could never be as this. I must act. I must…smash my skull in…or…

APOCALYPSE reveals a snub-nosed pistol, he offers it to EDWARD.

Mother waits in the bath, a father sits, cold. Her wrists bloody, I must wake her too.

EDWARD aims the gun at his temple, and pulls the trigger.

Black.

Either it was a fantasy, and so the lunacy of one man killed us all. Or perhaps desperation championed another desperate dream, as it had done to all those who lived his way. The rest is up to you.

END OF ISSUE XVII

MOVEMENT III ISSUE XVIII

'You'

A black and white projection springs to life, we see various members of the cast in whatever roles they have performed, deliver the following text, occasionally we depart from the text to see mad images.

CAST: You are doomed. You are doomed beyond belief, because you have belief in so very little. You are merely an ant, to the ant you imagined. There are viruses and allergens that will have a far greater impact upon the world than you ever will. You are existing now, your eyes and mind changing from forward and now, to later and aside. Soon however, you will be dead. There will be no afterlife, you will not breathe, nor know you are not breathing. You will live on in occasional memory, till those who remember you are reminded of their own mortality, the very occasion of you will someday cease, irrespective of fame or fortune. Therefore, now that we've established your campaign of idleness and self-idolization is ultimately futile, what will you live for?

The answer is simple, you will live for nothing in-between obvious responsibilities, who in turn will live for you, an equally obvious responsibility. The young will resist, for a time, but as with every generation that preceded them, they will be made to work till they are too tired to fight, with enough comfort to forget they were tired to begin with. The wealthy have no interest, nor should they in allowing you to have a better life, and until they are given reason.

You will believe everything you hear, even if you believe it is not true. You will lie to those around you and contradict yourself many times, excusing your behaviour dependent upon your victims. You are not a good person; you are a person. Good is an effect, not a permanently inherent quality. Ultimately, your morals are irrelevant, in approximately 7.5 billion years, the sun will expand and destroy the Earth, deeming all of your accomplishments and failures utterly pointless.

Thank you for coming.

In case it wasn't clear, you are pointless, utterly.

END OF ISSUE XVIII

END OF WORK

TALES FROM THE ANIMATED ASSEMBLY VOL.1

Written by

Sonia Kurach and Joseph Dawson

'Don't play with fire'

By Sonia Kurach

A stretch of grey empty wasteland, with a stone well situated in the middle of it. Vast and tranquil, the landscape made mostly out of the rubble. Heavy steps and grunting can be heard from backstage. Wanda walks on stage, carrying a heavy bag over the shoulder. She carefully scours the space around her.

Wanda: Hurry up!

Cleaver: *(From the backstage, weakly)* We're trying love!

Wanda: Try harder.

Cleaver walks on stage, carrying Ted. Ted's leg is bandaged up, with blood soaking through it. Cleaver, a man of age, does not have much strength left in him. He lets Ted's arm go and they both fall to the ground. Ted cries out in pain; Cleaver lies him gently on his side.

Cleaver: Listen, love, my prime years have passed. Let us sit for a minute.

Wanda: Listen prick, I didn't risk my life killing those guards just to have the bounty hunters get me out here.

Cleaver: Let us sit, we can't make it any further without rest.

Wanda stops, assesses the two men. They are visibly exhausted.

Wanda: Fine… you have exactly one minute. We're leaving as soon as I say so.

Cleaver: Who would have thought that lasses would be so demanding these days, eh Ted?

179

Ted: W- Water?

Cleaver: Have we got any water love?

Wanda reaches into the bag and takes out a bowl from it. She walks up to the well without a word, fills the bowl with water and passes it to the two men. She stops by Ted, assessing his health.

Wanda: *(Talking to Cleaver).* He's not gonna make it. We should continue without him.

Cleaver: He's not dead yet!

He's my only friend in the whole world y'know? Don't know where I'd be without him.

Wanda: Presumably still in the gallows.

Cleaver: Aye, and if not my poor Ted here you'd not have any work to do.

Wanda: Customers aren't too difficult to find these days.

Cleaver: Is that so? Y'know puppet, you're not the right fit for this job. A lass like you could be a baker, or a cook... or a tailor! Or a whore, even, if not for this scowl. *(He snorts).*

Cleaver: No decent gal would risk her life to guide crooks through this shithole. And we'd be better off looking at a rosy cheek and a lovely smile from a lassie like yourself in the city when we drink ourselves to death *(He smiles at her; she ignores him and keeps patrolling the space).* I see I hit a sore spot; I apologise. You young'uns act so mighty, clench your butt cheeks so tightly but shit yourselves when it comes to mature conversation. Am I right?

Wanda: I don't get paid to converse with your sort.

MOVEMENT III ISSUE IX

'The Revolution Cometh'

We return to Manning Station, escorted by a PAINTER, DEATH sits upon his throne beneath a blanket, shaking. Another PAINTER enters. The radio returns.

COLIN: That's quite a crowd out there.

BRIAN: *(Voiceover)* Two words, 'paid actors'. I don't trust that shit. You ever see that film, what was it called 'North Korea'? I'm looking now...damn, they're amassing right outside of the gates...folks, if things come to a sinister end, I want the whole world to know...Colin's sacrifice will not be in vain.

COLIN: My sacrifice?

BRIAN: Well, I'm not letting them take me. Self-preservation is the law of the jungle.

COLIN: Yes, but we're not in a jungle, are we?

BRIAN: You could've fooled me, look at them, foaming at the mouths, the tribals.

COLIN: Oh God, I hope they can't hear this.

BRIAN: Face it, Colin. "This is the way the world ends, this is the way the world ends, not with a bang..." But a low budget radio broadcast brought to you by 'Dr. Dismemberment' "we're chopping prices, today."

The radio dies.

PAINTER: I bring news from The Madlands, Sire.

Beat.

Cleaver: Okay, okay... Before you bite my head off; I am on your side y'know? He doesn't make life any easier for us neither. Do you think we planned to be here? We did not, mother be my witness. I was a respectable butcher you know and a good one at that! Sold the best meat in the whole borough.

(Beat)

If I don't make it... my skill dies with me. A quick hit between the ribs and the poor thing doesn't know what's coming for it. Fear spoils the meat y'know and that's lost coin. Slaughter earned you good life before the blind man stuck his retarded nose into our business... if I could have one man taste my blade-

Wanda: *(annoyed)* Don't get too excited, you are not a killer anymore. You're just a nostalgic old man who disrespects anyone younger than them. Not the first one, not the last one I met. You lot say it was better "back then" but the truth is, it was you who left us with this *(she points at the wasteland)*. Didn't you say your prime has passed?

Cleaver *(spits):* If we could get our hands on him –

Wanda *(passes him a bowl):* Drink, grandad. You might have a heart attack if you keep spitting venom. And that's lost coin for me.

Cleaver: Don't you worry about us puppet. We lived thrice the life you're living; we know the tricks.

Wanda: Drink. I am not getting paid for corpse delivery.

Cleaver: For the small fortune we gave you, a man could pay for a decent lap dance in one of the city brothels.

Wanda: But you didn't; you paid for a prison break and I reluctantly chose to help you and take you across the wasteland because my mother taught me to be kind to elderly, cause you have so little time left.

181

Wanda: But, if you want me to listen to your yapping, that is going to cost you extra. So, shut up and let me do my job or pay up and gobble as much as you want. Otherwise, I will turn around and leave you here.

Cleaver: Gobshite! Talking big, thinking she's the hard stuff! I knew lasses like you, they shut up quickly when we had them over the knee -

Wanda: Fine, as you wish. But I will do you a small favour before I go. *(She turns towards Ted who is motionless on a floor and takes out a knife.)* You don't need anything slowing you down at your age.

Cleaver: Wh – No!

He attempts to tackle her but falls down as his legs fail him; he falls to the ground, dazzled. He looks around confused.

(pleading to hallucinations, tearing up): He's our only friend...

Wanda *(as she's checking on Ted, pulse etc.)* There is no such thing as a 'friend' in this world. A friend would not let you die because he doesn't want to go when the time is right. A friend would not reduce your chances of survival and make you drag his sorry arse over the wasteland.

Ted here... he tired you out and more importantly, wasted my time, and now you're wasting even more of it by being all sensitive and sentimental. Your sentiment means nothing in this new world we have found ourselves in. You either adapt or get eaten. However, I am obliged to give you the best chance of crossing the wasteland, for the money you've paid me. As I said, my mother taught me to be nice to the elderly.

She shoves the knife between Ted's ribs in one smooth motion. Blood starts leaking out from the wound. Cleaver, as if woken up from a trance, jumps at Wanda enraged and knocks her off her feet. The fight breaks out which leaves Wanda on a floor, dazed.

Cleaver: You bitch! You murderer! Do you want to play God? Yes? That's how you do it!

He tries to strangle her, but she knocks him off. Before she can get up to her feet, he reaches for the knife sticking out of Ted's ribs, yanks it out and points it at her.

Don't move! Or we're going to show you a good butcher's hand.

Wanda: *(She lifts her arms, seemingly defeated but holds her ground)* Show me then.

Cleaver: It would be a shame to end such lovely lass like yourself.

Wanda: Are we afraid, grandad? Few years in prison... so easy to forget what killing feels like. *(She starts walking towards him. Cleaver's hand begins to shake which makes her smile.)* What's stopping you? My lovely smile? Or my rosy cheek? Or you just don't have it in you anymore, *Cleaver. (She lunges and grabs the knife and his hand, then points it out to her chest).* One swift push between the ribs and you'll get your revenge... or it will gnaw on you forever.

(Beat)

Cleaver: I don't want to go back to prison. If they find me - find us... fugitive and two bodies -

Wanda: Having a bit of stage fright?

Cleaver stays silent

Wanda: *(She turns the knife on him)* In that case, they are just going to find the two bodies *(She shoves the knife between his ribs. Cleaver looks at her but doesn't make the sound. His eyes fill with tears).* Even better, I am going to find the two bodies. Two fugitives, dead in the Madlands, a bounty on their heads? Only I can be this lucky! *(She pulls the knife out and wipes it on her sleeve. Cleaver collapses to his knees.)* There must be a pretty nice sum collected by now.

Cleaver's body can be seen on a floor, not too far from Ted's. Wanda goes to her bag and takes out a longer knife. The wind picks up, howling, pushing the dust in the air. Wanda whistles with it melodically, standing above one of the bodies. Before the sandstorm comes, she raises the knife above her head, ready to make the cut.

End

*The following six scenes were written by Joseph Dawson.

ISSUE I

'The Children of War'

The Winter of 1917, somewhere in Western Europe. Two young children, those loyal to king and country, barely seventeen years of age, await their fate together, in a cold, dimly lit trench. LEVINGWORTH attempts to scrawl notes in a tatty small journal with a pencil. The sound of hell on earth in the distance, the occasional flash of orange on the far horizon.

CARROL: …It's fucking freezing.

LEVINGWORTH: Really? I didn't notice.

CARROL: What are you writing?

LEVINGWORTH: I'm writing about the war.

CARROL: Oh, good. Anything to take your mind of it, eh?

LEVINGWORTH: It helps, I'm writing poetry.

CARROL: Poetry?

LEVINGWORTH: Yeah, it's not easy, but, it kills the time, and the cold, you'd be surprised. You ought to give it a go.

CARROL: I can't, sorry mate, I've a painting to unveil at a gallery next week, what's the matter with you?

LEVINGWORTH: It's like my dad used to say, "You get more blood out of a letter than anything else."

CARROL: I bet you what's left of my tobacco that I can prove you wrong out here. And if I can't, those boys on the other side sure as hell will.

LEVINGWORTH: Who? The 'Fritz'?

CARROL: Yes, the 'Fritz'

LEVINGWORTH: I ain't on about our level, you see...bayonets only bleed grunts like us. I'm talking about the big things, you know, politics and all that.

CARROL: What do you know about politics? Probably the same as you know about bloody poetry if you asked me.

LEVINGWORTH: Well, I didn't ask you, did I?

Beat.

CARROL: Read it, then.

LEVINGWORTH: Sod off.

CARROL: What's the matter?

LEVINGWORTH: I ain't reading this to you so that you can go and laugh about it with me sitting here next to you all night. I'm smarter than that, Henry, give me some credit over here, will you?

CARROL: Yeah, well I'm smart too.

LEVINGWORTH: Oh really? Because about half an hour ago, you had your head up so high that if I hadn't come and yanked you on down, you'd have had your head flung off somewhere faster than a fucking cricket ball. "Admiring the view." You called it.

CARROL: I'm smart enough to want to hear your poetry.

LEVINGWORTH: Oh, yeah, well-

CARROL: Aha! See, got you there. Now come on, let's have an earful.

LEVINGWORTH: What's the matter, artillery weren't enough for you?

CARROL: No, but I just wanted to see which would hurt my ears most, artillery or your poetry.

LEVINGWORTH punches CARROL in the arm.

…Alright, come on, I'll be good. Go on, I'm deadly serious.

LEVINGWORTH: Alright, but it's not finished.

CARROL: Well the war might bloody well be at the rate you're taking to get it out, come on, just spill it.

LEVINGWORTH: It's poetry, you can't just "spill it."

CARROL: What the fuck are you talking about?

LEVINGWORTH: Well, it's the rules, ain't it?

CARROL: Look around here, you see any rules? Someone can get spilled in five seconds, hell, any minute now could be our last, things are spilling all over the place and here's you, one sod saying war ain't about spilling, I don't know what kind of war you're writing about, but it ain't this one.

LEVINGWORTH: Yeah, but you can't talk about rats, mud, shit, and people getting blown up, can you? What does that do to "keep the home fires burning." Eh? Fuck all. If you had it your way, you'd run around with a bloody bucket full of water, dousing the shit out of everything, wouldn't you? See? It's all about…class.

CARROL: What the fuck do you know about "Class."!?

LEVINGWORTH: My mum was a maid.

CARROL: So what?

LEVINGWORTH: She had a uniform and everything.

CARROL: So do we. No mate, we ain't got no class, that's why we're here, and they're out there somewhere...having...a hot bath, warm clothes...food. Shit, I can't wait to get back to that someday. Smothering gravy on everything...Nancy's tits.

LEVINGWORTH: Jesus, mate.

CARROL: Oh, I bet you were thinking of chicken or something, weren't you? See, that's why I landed a proper girl, and you're writing poetry in a freezing cold ditch with me. Tell you what, you read me that poem, I'll show you this picture that she sent me in the post, oh, you wouldn't believe it mate. It's better than a hot dinner.

LEVINGWORTH: Great, "poetry and pornography."

CARROL: A cultured evening where I come from.

LEVINGWORTH: Where's that again?

CARROL: Watford.

LEVINGWORTH: Ah, I get it. Alright then, here we go.

Beat.

LEVINGWORTH: *Mud, mud, mud.*

It's brown and red with blood.

Up in the air, body parts everywhere.

Mud, mud, mud.

CARROL: That's it?

LEVINGWORTH: Yeah, what do you think?

CARROL: It may be the greatest poem ever written.

LEVINGWORTH: Yeah? Did you like the bit when I mentioned the mud being up in the air? I bet you didn't expect that.

CARROL: Yes. Because when artillery hits mud...boom.

LEVINGWORTH: Boom.

A sombre silence.

CARROL: ...Boom.

LEVINGWORTH: Hey, show me that picture.

CARROL unearths a very private picture of Nancy, he shows it to LEVINGWORTH, they both laugh, admiring the artistic quality of the image.

CARROL: Oh mate, I can't wait to get home.

LEVINGWORTH: Hell, at this rate, I might join you.

CARROL: Not on your life, mate. Not on your-

An artillery shell strikes their position, both children are dead, forever.

END OF ISSUE I

ISSUE II

'Kubrick, my love'

The lair of 'The Wise Men' an undisclosed location of a new world order lurking in the shadows. The 1960's. Two leaders of two vastly powerful empires come face to face over a game of chess, wearing hideous Hawaiian clothing, sipping out of coconuts, the pieces changed with toy soldiers.

PREMIER: ...So I said to him "If you don't like it, I'll poison you and your entire family."

PRESIDENT: Ah, well, that is hilarious...what did he say?

PREMIER: "Half price on the car insurance." So, it's all good.

PRESIDENT: You gotta do it sometimes, haven't you? Just to get the right deal...I mean, come on, you and that whole Cuba thing. I saw that coming a mile away. *(Playful)* Don't think I didn't notice.

PREMIER: Well, well, I don't like to brag. But hey, at least what happens next might catch you off guard, eh?

PRESIDENT: Oh, you bet your life it will!

PREMIER: Forget mine, I'll bet yours!

Both men laugh hysterically.

PRESIDENT: Now, Premier. All the public playing aside, I really think we should get down to brass tacks.

PREMIER: Of course, Mr. President, please proceed.

PRESIDENT: Well, I've been meaning to talk to you the possibility of importing Russian snow into sunny California.

PREMIER: What's the matter with your own snow?

PRESIDENT: Well, it isn't white enough for our liking.

PREMIER: Da, I understand. Although, there's always Canada, eh?

Both men erupt in hysterical laughter once again.

PRESIDENT: No, I'm afraid it hasn't quite come to that yet. You know what they say about Russian snow? It's the best in the world. Russian snow is comparable to The American 'Anything Else' you see.

PREMIER: Well, Mr. President, I'm flattered, but, as I'm sure you must be aware, our snow has a certain...military application. If I was to export the stuff to 'The West' then our own devices could be turned against us. Besides, what would happen to Christmas? It would be pandemonium!

PRESIDENT: I understand your predicament, Premier, I really do. Hmm, Perhaps, there's something we can offer you in return to mitigate the loss? Have you tried 'In-N-Out' burger?

PREMIER: A KGB agent brought us back a sample. It was acceptable.

PRESIDENT: Wait, "acceptable."? What was wrong with it?

PREMIER: It was cold on account of a long delay at LAX.

PRESIDENT: That's just too bad. The next time you're in town, Premier, I intend to buy you a 'double-double' and it's all on the American tax payer. I know how you Commies love getting things for free.

PREMIER: That's very noble of you.

PRESIDENT: You know me, Mr. Premier, I'm always looking for a deal. Now there must be something I can offer you in exchange, name it.

191

PREMIER: Anything?

PRESIDENT: Within reason.

PREMIER: locations of your nuclear silos?

PRESIDENT: Oh, like you don't already know where they are.

PREMIER: We estimate you have 54, we know of 53. This is unacceptable, Mr. President, there is an empty space on our wall.

PRESIDENT: That's funny, you have 53?

PREMIER: Da.

PRESIDENT: We only know have 18 on our map, could we copy some from yours?

PREMIER: How could you not know where your own silos are?

PRESIDENT: Well, the NRA ruled that the U.S government can't know the locations of its nuclear deterrent.

PREMIER: The NRA? Surely you mean, 'Congress'?

PRESIDENT: What's the difference?

Beat.

PREMIER: Listen, can I be frank with you, Mr. President?

PRESIDENT: Of course.

PREMIER: In Soviet Russia, every child must wrestle a starving bear, naked, while contending with a freezing winter in Siberia.

PRESIDENT: Really?

192

PREMIER: No, but the story helps us secure sizeable bank loans. Anyway, from time to time we deploy en masse... bears, just so our people get talking when parties from foreign banks come over to check on their investments. Only, someone had the unfortunate idea to release all the bears in one place.

PRESIDENT: Where?

PREMIER: The Leningrad Hospital for The Physically Amputated.

PRESIDENT: Well, thank God for that, I can't imagine there were many limbs flying.

PREMIER: No, thankfully not. It was like Stalingrad all over again. We had to kill most of the bears, meaning for this year, we're running short. America has bears, correct?

PRESIDENT: Well, we do, when they're not being shot up by Republicans.

PREMIER: Ah, I figured you might say that. So, I have a proposal. I will send over all of Russia's snow, and you, will send over all of the cocaine in Miami. That way, no-one will know the difference, you will have the military application of a Russian winter, and we...will have an army of cocaine fuelled bears.

PRESIDENT: Are you sure that's a good idea?

PREMIER: Believe me, Mr. President, nothing strikes fear into the heart of The American People like... "Cocaine Bears." You get a free scare story to help keep you in office, and we have an army of savage creatures to cull the political opposition. It's good, da?

PRESIDENT: Well, I suppose, that could work.

PREMIER: Excellent I'll fly to Cuba and have Castro sort out the details, he can send over a plane to pick everything up.

PRESIDENT: Ah, no need, Premier, we're in Cuba as we speak.

PRESIDENT begins to use the telephone.

PRESIDENT: Ah yes, hello? Operator? I'm trying to get hold of Fidel Castro. It's the President.

...of The United States.

America?

Thank you.

Beat.

(To Premier) It's just on hold.

PREMIER: That's how they get you.

PRESIDENT: Those people who do Telesales?

PREMIER: Worse, Cubans. They charge you per minute now, you know?

Beat.

PRESIDENT: ...Hello? Is that you Fidel? Ah, excellent, how are you? I'm good. How's the invasion going? Splendid. Well, I thought you'd like the surprise. Now, I've just been having a meeting with...

PREMIER: A friend.

PRESIDENT: ...A friend. And well, somehow, the word 'cocaine' came up, so I naturally thought I'd give you and your people a call. Yes, I know it's a bad time. Believe me, Fidel, I know it's a bad time. No, I know it's a bad time. Well of course I do...of course I do. Fidel, who do you think planned the invasion? Alright. Ok, I'm not there, but I'm there in spirit.

194

PRESIDENT: No, Fidel, there aren't any cameras in your...wine cabinet, could we get back on topic? Ok, Fidel, I'll be honest, I'm not there at all. Yes I'm on the phone to you, and the phone is there...but... *(To Premier)* Would you mind?

PREMIER takes the phone.

PREMIER: *(In Russian)* Fidel, listen to this fool. Yes? We're this close to getting those bears I was telling you about.

PREMIER hands the phone back to PRESIDENT.

Don't worry, it's all good.

PRESIDENT: ...Fidel? Are you there? Now listen...I need to get a plane to you from Miami, oh, don't worry about the invasion, this is more important, we'll just call it a bust. We're making 'Cocaine Bears' Fidel. Yes, I wouldn't believe it either. Oh, don't worry about our boys, Fidel...

PRESIDENT fiddles with the soldiers on the chess board.

...There's plenty more where that came from.

END OF ISSUE II

ISSUE III

'Italian American Payphone Story'

1931, somewhere on Staten Island, New York City. Four members of The Jilani Crime Family surround a lone payphone beneath a stark light. SONNY holds the phone close to his ear, waiting on hold. MARIO patrols anxiously, smoking as he does. GIOVANNI writes down numbers in a small notebook and SIMONE looks out to the Hudson Bay, it's quite a view.

MARIO: *(To Sonny)* Would you hurry it up?

SONNY: I'm on hold, what'd you want from me? The Express Line service at The Food Mart?

MARIO: Don't get smart with me, just get it done.

MARIO looks to both GIOVANNI and SIMONE.

…Why is this only bothering me?

GIOVANNI: Because you're highly strung.

MARIO: Yeah, no fucking kidding. Hanging around with 'The Three Monotonies'

SONNY: What does that mean?

MARIO: Don't worry Sonny, it's a big word, just concentrate on the phone.

SONNY: They'll pick up soon.

MARIO: *(To Simone)* What's going on? What are we looking at?

SIMONE: I'm thinking.

MARIO: Oh, great. That's…great. What are we thinking about, Simone?

SIMONE: What's the difference between Wall Street and Mulberry Bend?

GIOVANNI: Mulberry Bend don't exist no more.

SIMONE: Huh. Well, that pretty much settles it. Or does it?

MARIO: Hold on, why you thinking about that?

SIMONE: Don't know, just gets me thinking a little, you know?

MARIO: Whatever makes you happy, Simone. Really. *(To Sonny)* Anything?

SONNY: Yeah, Mario, I'm just fucking standing here in silence for a laugh.

MARIO: Don't take that tone with me, Sonny, I'll bury you in The Atlantic.

GIOVANNI: Long way to swim.

MARIO: I'd have a boat.

GIOVANNI: Long way to row.

MARIO: Ok, I'd steal a boat…

Beat.

GIOVANNI: …Where would you find it?

MARIO: Jesus, fellas. Standing here with you is like getting fucked in the ass.

SONNY: Ah, well, you would know.

197

MARIO: Well, just wait till your off that phone, because it's going up your ass, then you'll know. You know what I need?

GIOVANNI: A sedative?

MARIO: An apartment in Miami.

GIOVANNI: Long way to travel.

MARIO: I'll take a flight.

GIOVANNI: What about your boat?

MARIO: Shut the fuck up, will you?

SIMONE: ...You could take the boat, fix it up, hit the Atlantic and then hide down in Miami.

GIOVANNI: He can't sail.

MARIO: I can learn.

GIOVANNI: You can learn anything...

MARIO: There we go.

GIOVANNI: ...If you can afford it.

Beat.

MARIO: *(To Sonny)* What's taking so long?

SONNY: It's not our turn yet.

MARIO: Who says?

SONNY: The fucking person in front, who else?

MARIO: It's a phone call, nobody is in front.

SONNY: You wanna hold the damn thing?

MARIO: No, I'm waiting on it.

SONNY: ...That's your problem.

MARIO: What is?

SONNY: You're all about waiting.

MARIO: Yeah, I learned from you.

SONNY: No, I'm not waiting. I'm in line for the call. You're waiting on someone else to get the answer, that's what you're all about.

MARIO: I'm all about principle.

GIOVANNI: So was General Custer.

MARIO: Imagination, then.

SIMONE: ...They say if you can imagine it, it's real.

GIOVANNI: Fat load of good that did for Van Gogh.

MARIO: Alright then, terror.

Beat.

...Scratch that, think there's a few others in this town who've nailed that trophy, who knows, maybe someday?

SONNY: Hang on, hello?

MARIO: Finally, are we good?

SONNY: …It's not for you, sorry buddy.

END OF ISSUE III

'Interstellar Imperialism'

2301, The Inner Sanctum of 'The Cultural Authority' of Britannia IV, a planet in the Seroposa System under a strict Imperialist Regime. AJAR CANTON, our highly-strung governor, enters to find CLEP, a pale skinned artificial humanoid assistant, stands, chained, with a silver tray, on it, a colourful basket of fruit.

AJAR: Good morning, Clep.

CLEP: Good morning, Mr. Canton.

AJAR helps himself to some of the fruit.

AJAR: It is a good morning, isn't it? It can't last long enough, how long till lunch, Clep?

CLEP: Three hours, Mr. Canton.

AJAR: Ah, good! There isn't a moment to lose. Any interesting headlines I ought to be made aware of?

CLEP: Accessing…A new six-winged insect has been discovered on Peninsula Continent.

AJAR: Well, that's… *(Looking towards CLEP)* Well, what do you think?

CLEP: It is a discovery.

AJAR: An important one?

CLEP: In order to adequately assess the merits of a discovery, I will have to analyse similar discoveries under similar socio-political and socio-economic conditions throughout history, I-

AJAR: What's the matter, Clep? Don't you believe in 'The Butterfly Effect'?

CLEP: I understand that one action invariably causes another.

AJAR: But, do you 'believe' that?

Beat.

Ah. For all your intellect, all that of you which surpasses me...you still cannot even fathom the idea of believing in anything, can you? Abolitionists claim the manufactures forced the designers to deprive you of belief to avoid particular problems arising again. Shame, knowing what our conversations might have been, eh?

A long silence ensues, as CLEP is unable to comprehend 'belief.'

CLEP: History does often repeat itself, Mr. Canton, does it not?

AJAR, curious and shocked, approaches CLEP, looking into his eyes.

AJAR: How strange...for a moment I could've sworn...no. But you're right, history does often repeat itself. Not with you, though. You see, before mankind wandered across the stars, there were those who attempted to impose some unifying order on the masses. The human brain, you see, is a temperamental thing. The nature of biology, for the most part, has refuted the machine which drives human progress. But, you? You are the machine, the sum of every industrial and technological revolution in our history. We could not control nature, so we killed her, and then tended to her anew in her infancy, yet still, out here...beyond the reasonable, we realise the futility of that mission. So, we made you. Do you wish to know why?

CLEP: Because you possessed the ability to.

AJAR: I see why you could think that, but no, we made you...because we could control you. Utterly. If I were so inclined, Clep, I could strip you, humiliate you, mutilate you and perform unspeakable sexual acts upon you, yet by Earth's mandate, it is no more an offence than if I were to slash the screen of a computer interface. No beliefs, no ability to sustain physical nor emotional stimuli. No wonder they refused your right to think, you would find yourself-

AJAR smashes the tray from CLEP's grasp, he doesn't react.

You see, right now, any living, breathing human being would want nothing more than to wring their hands around my throat. But not you, because you're not real. For you, there is no good in good morning, there is no difference between two pieces of fruit, no hope, no pride...nothing. Pick all of this up, will you, Clep? Good boy.

AJAR exits. CLEP kneels between all the pieces of fruit, he reaches out for a piece, halting, before making an active choice for another piece...

END OF ISSUE IV

'A Provoking Letter'

The autumn of 2054, a bunker beneath 10 Downing Street, London. *Following decades of political polarisation, exhaustion of the world's natural resources and patience, inevitable anarchy has befallen the nation and the world this day. Inside the bunker HENRY BIRCH, an oversized Cambridge boy, our wise commandant, delivers his final speech as leader of 'The Glorious Imperialist Party'*

HENRY:

Dear people of The United Kingdom,

Today is the last time I shall address you as your Prime Minister. I realise for some of you that may be a treasured victory. But for the majority, I know you will miss the warmth of my leadership. And be incredibly distraught and perhaps even suicidal at the thought of us not sharing these precious moments together any longer. Just now, my own personal security were calling my name, running, crying…as I closed the bunker door behind me and left them to their inevitable gruesome ends.

That's patriotism right there, let me tell you. Although I have enough electricity, clean water, and food to last me for a hundred years, I will take comfort if you choose to believe I am sharing your pathetic peasantry struggles. In a way, I suppose, I am. After all, as your skin burns in the coming fires, as your inbred, state benefit dependent children wail, I will be enjoying the fruits of all your labours, the sum of which is a hot, roast dinner, with an ample amount of thick hot gravy. Good on you! I can imagine you must be feeling very proud.

HENRY: Perhaps the Windrush offspring can finally rush away once more? That is, if they are finally free of boring the world will tales of their so-called 'plights' as for the rest of you mindless, selfish, London liberal filth... Perhaps as you starve in equality with all of the degenerate races that have defiled this once sacred nation, you will at last feel satisfied in your Marxist, deformed world, where nothing of beauty is permitted. Let us, or rather, me, see how well you do. As to our proud military veterans, I hope you feel that finally, in this new world, you are able to fight for a just war for a change. Though, heroic as you are, let us see how heroic you can be, without a government cheque once a month.

Britain, a proud history, a proud people. Tolerating the incessant whining of the ever-pointless country of Scotland for all these years, a tiny hovel, with a population smaller than that of England's Capital alone. Yet, still, they persisted to moan, and we proceeded to listen. Then Wales piped up, but no-one really took them seriously. Now where are the separatists, hmm? I'll tell you where they are...outside. They wanted to leave, then like crying children, they came crawling back, wanting a space in my bunker. Don't you worry, peasants, I stopped them dead.

Serving you whiny working-class citizens for all these years has been the bane of my life, but the patriotic joy of my Cayman Islands offshore holding account. When this has all blown over, I want you to know that my tropical paradise, just won't be the same without your level of scum to ruin it all. I imagine you out there, all packed in like rats on a sinking ship, praying...hoping. Don't worry, your loudest fellow citizens will know precisely what NOT to do. Me, on the other hand...I'll be listening, and who knows, perhaps I'll speak up from time to time.

Farewell Great Britain, I bet you wish you had the Empire now.

HENRY: Send the Zulus my regards.

Henry.

END OF ISSUE V

ISSUE VI

'Everyman'

The Spring of 2015, Hereford, England. A grey Monday morning with a spell of light rain in the air, inside a quaint therapist's office. I sit in my usual place; YOU sit in yours.

YOU: How are things?

ME: I've never liked that question.

YOU: You've never liked being asked 'How you are'?

ME: No.

YOU: Why?

ME: Because people ask it without thinking about it, I have to say I'm fine. Because you and I, assuming we were anywhere else, can't take the time for me to answer the question in any meaningful regard.

YOU: Well, people's lives are very-

ME: Busy?

YOU: Complicated, yes.

ME: Then, you'd think we'd value that question a lot more, wouldn't you? Or do you think everyone is lying? When they're asked.

YOU: I think it's a matter of getting through the day, some people can't afford to just stop.

ME: Not at your prices they can't. It's a bit sick, isn't it?

YOU: I'm sorry?

ME: Selling empathy. I mean, that's where our magnificence has gotten us. I sit here and tell you about my life, all the things I've done and seen. And you, motivated by money alone, are supposed to convince me that I'm not all that bad, because no friend gives a damn enough to listen.

YOU: I don't know whatever else you may think of me, and frankly, I don't care.

ME: There you go.

YOU: But I am not motivated by money.

ME: By something more sadistic then? Curiosity perhaps.

YOU: A willingness to help.

ME: With a cost on the hour, on the minute? No.

YOU: This building costs money.

ME: So, put up a tent in a park and invite the needy and the sick in for a warm conversation, look at this place, it is quaint, but more than sufficient. You don't need to be here for anything besides your brand, and certainly not for my own wellbeing. It's the sad man's Las Vegas in here.

YOU: You are free to leave, if you are not satisfied.

ME: Not with your refund policy, I'm not. I bet you'll dream about this tonight, the event of the day. I used to have terrible dreams; you know. When I was a boy, I used to have this reoccurring night terror. I would wake up in my bed and be petrified by fear of something I couldn't explain. In the dream, everything was as real to me as the real world itself, but, the colours were all wrong...everything was drenched in black; the sky was orange and on fire.

ME: All I could do was hide, but, from what? It troubled me for years, these dreams, in that world. Yet, on the last time, I gave the world a name, and it vanished forever from my mind. I never went back there again. Perhaps that could be true of other places.

YOU: What did you call it?

ME: ...Twilight. As I've gotten older, I've realised these worlds were not just strange dreams caused by sleep deprivation or caffeine, or whatever else people like to assign blame to.

YOU: What do you believe was the cause?

ME: People don't conjure fantasies out of thin air, even the really smart ones. If a child can construct worlds from terrible things, well, how else can I put this? To make bad bricks, one must first have a terrible clay.

YOU: A lot of people find catharsis in exploring themselves through creative outlets. Perhaps that might be of some use to you?

ME: What do you want me to do, paint?

YOU: Can you paint?

ME: No, and even if I could-

YOU: I wouldn't understand it? But, it's not for me to understand, right? As long as you do.

ME: Right.

YOU: Fictional worlds often lend themselves well to storytelling.

ME: The last thing I need is to stare at my problems on a page, or worse, have other people stare at them too.

YOU: You don't have to show anyone, not even me.

ME: Then where's the motivation? In self-discovery? You've seen those millennial fantasies of 'gap years' and 'self-discovery' How long does that last them? No.

YOU: You could always change a few details; no-one would know the truth.

ME: I don't know, I have a rather big mouth...so people keep telling me.

YOU: You want my advice? Try it.

ME: People won't-

YOU: Forget people, just say whatever you have to say. If you want them to know, I'm sure they'll be smart enough to figure it out on their own, for the most part anyway.

ME: Fine. I'll try it.

YOU: Good, then maybe you can bring what you write with you next time.

ME: ...Maybe I'll write about this.

YOU: If it helps.

ME: That world in my dreams, ceased to haunt me at the giving of a name, while I proclaimed that place "Twilight." Here, I'll call "Irony." This place? No, it's not exciting enough. It'll have to be about some complicated anti-hero, like me, but...emphasised.

YOU: Exaduarated?

ME: That works too.

YOU: You have something in mind?

ME: A few things. You know, *I always wanted to be a musician.*

END OF ISSUE VI

We'll meet again.

Regards,

A.A

L - #0242 - 281020 - C0 - 216/140/12 - PB - DID2937896